Call Sign Panther

Andy Jones

ISBN 978-1-3999-2481-8

www.andrewmjones.co.uk

"I'm reporting to 506 Squadron." I replied quickly and produced the set of papers with my orders on.

"Smith can run you over in the wagon, he's just finishing his tea. Wanna sling your stuff in the back?" He pointed to a short wheelbase Bedford lorry, which was parked outside. Before I'd left the room he was back in full flow explaining how his sister-in-law was the root cause of his marital issues.

I placed my luggage in the lorry and walked around to wait by the passenger door. The Bedford was a square looking machine painted serge blue to match the uniforms we wore. Hand painted in white letters was the serial number. Judging by its paintwork I assumed the vehicle was fairly new, but I noticed that the passenger side wheel arch was badly dented and a series of deep gashes ran down the side of the cab. I don't believe I'd ever seen a damaged service vehicle before then. I'd spent months being marched up and down operational training units, where everything was ordered and tidy. This, however, was an active fighter station in the middle of a battle, where keeping the airfield clear of bomb craters was far more important than painting the picket fence outside station headquarters.

I looked at my reflection in the passenger window, straightened my tie and adjusted the position of my forage cap. The damn thing never sat right. On the recruiting posters those caps always looked so dynamic, but on my head it seemed to accentuate my thin face and make me look even younger.

A door slammed behind me and someone who I assumed to be Smith appeared.

"506?" he said as if he was a cabby asking which train I was catching.

Smith was definitely not a natural driver. He lurched the lorry forward and onto the road which ran behind a large green aircraft hangar. By the way he handled the gear lever I imagined he'd have been happier shovelling coal into the boiler of a tramp steamer.

North Weald was an airfield set into the Essex countryside, about twenty miles north east of London. It was one of a series of fighter stations that formed a defensive ring around the capital. With the threat of invasion hanging over the country North Weald, like all of these stations, was buzzing with activity.

Everywhere I looked there were groups of people. There were squads of khaki clad soldiers, officers on pushbikes, clerks with paper files stuffed under their arms, everyone appeared to have an urgent purpose.

A bright red MG sports car overtook us, Smith jerked the gears again and we continued on past another hangar. Here, outside in the bright sunshine, sat a Hawker Hurricane. The engine cowlings had been removed revealing the black mass of the Rolls Royce engine. A fitter on a set of precarious wooden steps was peering into the airframe while on top of the wing two other men wrestled with a long belt of ammunition that sparkled in the sunlight. I was taken aback for a second. In all my training I'd had little gunnery practise and never seen such a large amount of live ammunition being loaded. I'd grown to love flying but almost forgotten the reason I was here, to fight.

We cut across between the next two hangars and suddenly the vast expanse of grass which made up the airfield was in front of us. The hangar doors were open and I peered in trying to make out the different types of aircraft that were being worked on.

On the edge of the concrete hardstanding another three Hurricanes were positioned facing the runway. A twin-engine Bristol Blenheim in its dark night fighter camouflage was being towed backwards by a Fordson tractor. Even with my training completed and over one hundred and fifty flying hours to my name, aircraft and airfields still brought out a boyish excitement in me.

We ran off the concrete onto a rough track which skirted the airfield perimeter. I noticed the red MG about fifty yards in front of us. Smith was unphased by the uneven road surface and kept the speed up. I clutched the door handle to prevent myself from bouncing off the seat as the potholes jolted through the chassis and I wondered if my luggage would still be with us when we stopped.

We were approaching a set of wooden huts outside of which more Hurricanes stood. Twelve in total, all belonging to 506 Squadron, the unit I'd been assigned to. My stomach tensed as I looked on wondering what to expect.

As we came nearer I could see a group of men outside of the Squadron Dispersal Hut. Some were sitting on a disorganised collection of seats. One lay on the ground with what looked like a parachute as a pillow and a few stood drinking from mugs.

The MG had pulled over and parked by the building. The driver sprung out and reached into the rear of the open top car. Smith slammed his foot down hard on the Bedford's brake pedal sending up a cloud of dust and grit towards the building. I slid forward and almost headbutted the dashboard.

The cloud dispersed and I saw the driver of the MG

striding towards my door. Behind him a layer of dust was settling on the bright red paint and polished chrome work of his car. I opened the door just as he reached us.

"You bloody idiot!" he yelled. "What are you doing crashing up here at that speed!"

Although his remarks were directed at Smith sitting alongside me, I shrunk into my own seat as though I was being scolded too. Smith gave a bemused look and then through gritted teeth uttered.

"Sorry Sir."

There was a momentary pause in which I seized the opportunity to slip out and retrieve my luggage. I heard a few more raised words and then the passenger door slammed shut. The group of men outside the building were now watching us. It wasn't the 'good first impression' I'd been planning on making.

In my embarrassment I'd avoided looking at the driver of the MG, but now as he walked back to his dust-covered car, I watched him. He was a tall, but not too lean officer. From behind I could see his uniform was well tailored and the car he drove suggested he had a private income additional to the monthly wage of a flight lieutenant.

Smith turned the lorry around and trundled down the track at a much more sedate speed. I picked up my luggage and walked to the building. It was wooden and similar in shape and size to a parochial village hall. The walls were clad in black painted timber and the corrugated roof was olive green. To prevent splinters from bomb blasts the iron frame windows had been taped with scrim, as had every pane of glass in southern England.

The door, which had seen several coats of gloss

paint, was ajar. Beside it a hand painted sign was balanced on a folding chair. Above a crest and motto it read '506 Squadron Royal Air Force'. Under the chair was a tin can with 'donations welcome' written in chalk. The can was empty.

I stepped inside and took off my cap. To the left was an office where I could hear the keys of a typewriter being rhythmically bashed. A sign hung on the door. 'Squadron Adjutant's Office.' I was about to knock, but before I could clench my fist the door flew open and a short tubby officer looked out towards me. His hair was parted to the side and swept back with a glossy coat of brilliantine.

"Er.., Hello, I'm to report to 506 Squadron...sir" I blurted out.

"Name?" he barked back.

"Sommers, sir."

"Good, report to the CO and I'll take your paperwork in a bit." He gestured to the next door where another sign hung. This one had a name and read 'Commanding Officer, Squadron Leader Hardy-Burton D.F.C.'

I replaced my cap and rubbed the toe of my shoes, where another layer of Smith's dust had settled, on the back of my calves, then knocked firmly on the door.

"Yes." A soft but firm voice drifted through the woodwork. I opened the door and took two steps into the office. It was a small room with a single wooden desk, two chairs and a filing cabinet. Just as the sign had promised behind the desk sat Squadron Leader Hardy-Burton D.F.C., or HB as he was familiarly known.

In front of him was a foolscap folder thick with yellow sheets of paper. His left hand held the folder open, while between the fingers of his right, a cigarette smouldered away. Judging by the length of the ash, the file had held his attention for some time. He didn't look up from the paper until I neatly clicked my heels together and snapped my arm up into a smart salute.

"Sergeant Sommers, reporting sir." He studied my face.

"Yes, I had a note you were arriving today." He flicked the ash into the tray. "Got your logbook there?"

"Yes sir, it's in my bag outside." I spun on my heels and made for my suitcase cursing the fact that I didn't have my logbook ready to present. When I returned to the office HB had risen from his chair and was staring out of the window towards the sky. It was a common pose that aviators adopted, you might well think they were deep in thought or daydreaming, in fact they were studying the weather. Looking at the way the clouds were forming and what that might mean for the next operation. I placed my pale blue logbook neatly on the table and stood back. He turned and picked it up.

"How many hours total?" By this he meant how many hours had I logged as a pilot.

"156, sir." He thumbed his way quickly through the neat pages.

A pilot's personal logbook is a detailed record of his flying career. All the types of aircraft he's flown, the airfields he'd flown from, the instructors he'd flown with and of course any mishaps or accidents he had along the way.

In many cases they are more accurate than his official service record and in later life they serve as an important aide-memoire whenever one feels nostalgic.

"And how many hours on Hurricanes?" he asked, as his thumb reached the last page of entries.

"19, sir." There was heavy silence as he scrutinised the handwritten entries and gave me no indication as to what he thought of my experience. A loud rap behind me broke the tension. I turned to see a dark haired pilot leaning through the door frame.

"Sorry to butt in skipper, but it's a quarter to," he said.

With one hand HB snapped the logbook shut and gave it back to me. From the chair alongside he picked up his flying helmet and stubbed his cigarette.

"You won't be flying today, and probably not tomorrow. The Adj will get your kit sorted. In the meantime get settled in." He pushed past me into the narrow corridor and out onto the airfield. The squadron pilots, who'd all witnessed my dust covered arrival, got to their feet as their Commanding Officer approached and formed a loose semi-circle around him.

"Right Gentlemen! Same as before, fifteen thousand feet and patrol the estuary between Foulness and Sheppey. Don't forget to keep an eye on your engine temperatures and make sure your oxygen is on. Any questions?" The twelve pilots remained silent. "Okay, airborne in five minutes."

On his words there was a flurry of activity. The fitters and riggers who'd appeared from one of the other buildings busied themselves with preparing the aircraft.

The pilots wrestled on their various pieces of flying gear. One of them, who'd forgotten some piece of kit, dashed towards the hut. I stepped outside to let him through, as I did so something bounded up to my ankle. It was a small dog, a Welsh Terrier, golden brown with a black saddle shaped patch on its back. It sniffed my trouser leg inquisitively and when it was satisfied I wasn't a threat, let me stroke its wiry coat.

"Hello boy, what's your name?" I asked.

"You'll really get in her bad books if you call her a boy." I was startled to find the Adjutant standing in the doorway watching me. He stepped out and bent down to greet the dog with an affectionate rub behind the ear.

"This is Mabel, she's the CO's and unofficial squadron mascot." He rose up and straightened his uniform tunic. "By the way, you're booked into the Sergeants' Mess. First thing tomorrow morning, draw what kit you need from the stores and report back here. I'm not sure what the CO has in mind for you yet, but it's best you hang around the crew room."

"Yes sir," I replied.

Mabel had now lost interest in us and wandered over to the empty chairs. I stood watching the squadron prepare itself. It was the first time I'd seen the pilots of 506. I would know some of those men for only a matter of weeks, and yet their names and faces would be ingrained in my memory for years to come.

Cavendish, the owner of the dust covered MG and well tailored uniform was already in the cockpit of his Hurricane. Alongside was Warwick, the second most senior officer.

'Lanky' Long, a sergeant pilot like myself, was being helped into his parachute harness. Ray Packard, an Australian who'd been given the imaginative nickname Aussie, was taking a last swig of tea from an enamel mug. Although looking back I'd imagine it was something stronger than tea. There was Hardy-

Chapter 2
Dress Regulations

That evening I booked into the Sergeants' Mess.
There were four sergeant pilots on the squadron.
Myself, 'Lanky' Long who towered over us at six foot
four inches. 'Freddie' Fuller who came from a family
of Cornish landowners and Tony Hill a quiet
Mancunian who kept himself to himself.

I'd been given an eight by twelve foot room to
share with Lanky Long. The room was a standard
affair, identical to hundreds of rooms all over the
world wherever Royal Air force personnel were
billeted. Two metal framed beds were pushed against
the wall, each with its own table. A narrow wooden
wardrobe was shared by both occupants. Cream lino
covered the floor and a thin square rug almost
provided a homely touch. It was sparse but much more
comfortable than living under canvas as many other
squadrons had been forced to.

Lanky lay sprawled on the bed reading a copy of
Popular Mechanics magazine. His large size eleven
feet hung over the end frame. It was a wonder how he
ever fitted in an aircraft.

"Have you been on the squadron long?" I asked as I
unpacked my suitcase. Lanky's eyes peeked at me
from over the colourful front cover.

"Only a few weeks. I joined them just after they
came back from France. I had a bad smash at the end
of last year which put me out of flying for a while."

I was brimming with questions about operational
flying.

"Have you seen much action?"

"Depends on what you call much action." Lanky lowered the magazine onto his stomach and sighed. "I've done a fair bit of stooging around the sky, but the nearest I've got to Jerry so far was yesterday, when we split up a flight of 88's." I detected a fair amount of frustration in his answer so I changed the subject. We discussed mealtimes, the weather and general living arrangements. He was polite and friendly, but we didn't have much in common. Sometimes that makes for a good roommate.

In the morning Lanky was up and gone before sunrise as the squadron was to patrol at first light. I woke about six thirty, dressed and drew back the blackout curtains. The sky was dreary with a low hanging layer of grey stratus clouds.

After breakfast I took a leisurely walk to the stores to draw the personal equipment I needed.

"Sign here," said the Stores Clerk and he thumped his forefinger down on the clipboard in front of me. I looked at the list of items.

1 Flying jacket, sheepskin lined, chest 38 inches.

1 Pair of flying boots, size 8.

1 Pair of pilot's gloves, leather.

1 Type 'B' flying helmet, size 3.

1 Set of flying goggles, (like the ones I'd found yesterday.)

1 Type 'D' oxygen mask with microphone fitted.

Alongside each item was its value which had been totalled up to thirty five pounds and 10 shillings. The clerk took delight in informing me that if I lost or damaged any of these items I was liable to pay for a replacement.

On my wage packet it would have taken about six months to pay that lot off. I mused over the fact that when I flew a Hurricane no one said that I'd be liable to pay for a replacement if the aircraft was lost or damaged. Typically the British bureaucrat was more concerned with a ten shilling pair of gloves than a ten thousand pound aircraft.

With the flying boots and helmet in one hand, the goggles and gloves tucked into my pocket and the jacket clamped under my other arm, I set off towards the squadron. I was making good progress towards the airfield when I heard someone shout.

"That man there!" It was such a shrill piercing shout that I turned to see what was going on. On the steps of the station headquarters stood a figure wearing a peaked cap and wielding a black pace stick. He stood rigid, his back forming a dead straight line from heel to head. On his wrist I could make out the coat of arms which identified him as a Warrant Officer, in this case the Station Warrant Officer or SWO.

"That man there!" he shouted again and I realised with horror he was addressing me. I stopped walking and turned to face him.

"Stand to attention!" he snapped and proceeded towards me with a fierce glint in his eyes. I was unable to stand to attention with all the equipment under my arms. I hesitated for a moment, but then decided to carry out his orders and with that let go of the jacket, boots and helmet. They fell into a heap on the tarmac. The SWO halted about two feet from my face. He assessed me with a quick scan of the eyes and noticed the pilot's brevet on my chest. I noticed the large collection of medals sewn on his.

He swung the pace stick round from under his arm and used it to point at me.

"You are improperly dressed." As he spoke, I felt a

cold breeze on my head. He was correct. In loading myself up with the flying equipment I'd forgotten to put on my forage cap, which was now lying on the roadside with everything else I dropped. I reached down, grabbed it and fixed it to my head. The action was all in vain though, the offence had already been committed. The SWO poked my stomach with the end of the pace stick and drew it up to my chest as if he was gutting a trout.

"I don't care what you lot do up there." He pointed a gnarled finger to the clouds. "But down here you're under my command." I got the feeling he wasn't too keen on pilots. From his tunic pocket he drew a tiny notepad and pencil.

"Name."

"Sommers."

"What squadron?" I was about to answer when a vehicle pulled up on the curb alongside us. It was a racing green three litre Bentley being driven by 'Mac' MacKay. In the passenger seat was another pilot, Flying Officer Barker. My morning couldn't get worse. It was bad enough to be reprimanded by the SWO, but now two of the squadron's officers had arrived.

"What's going on here Mr Murray?" Mac asked as he leaped out of the Bentley.

"This man was improperly dressed. Walking past the station headquarters without appropriate headgear."

"Right, I'll take things from here." Mac stared at me with a furious expression.

Murray spoke again. "I was going to…."

"Thank you, Mr Murray!" Mac interrupted him while keeping his eyes fixed on me "We will not tolerate bad standards in this squadron!" I shrunk inside, I hadn't been on the station for twenty four hours and I'd already arrived in a cloud of dust and broken Kings Regulations. Murray put his notepad and pencil away. Mac turned towards him.

"Thank you." He said firmly. The SWO saluted smartly and walked on past me. Mac came closer and whispered to me.

"Stay dead still." I did as I was told. Behind me I could hear the clip, clip, clip of the warrant officer's highly polished shoes getting fainter. Mac's face broke into a beaming smile. I stood to attention, completely confused.

"Come on, grab your gear I'll give you a lift." He bent down and picked up my jacket. "Don't worry about Murray. He's a relic of the Great War. I think he'd be happier marching up and down Chelsea Barracks, God knows why he's in the air force."

I turned to check that Murray had gone and then picked up my boots and helmet. Barker took them from me and stowed them on the rear seat.

"There's a few old goats like that around," he said. "They're harmless, but best to keep on the right side of them." The Bentley was an enormous car. It sat high on four large wheels which meant getting in was challenging. A thick aluminium step engraved with a letter 'B' protruded from the chassis and gave enough height for me to swing my leg over and land in the rear seat. Mac bounded into the front with a lot more grace. I noticed the floor was made from plywood and stained with mud and oil. By my feet were a selection of spanners, a tin of grease and a few other tools.

I assumed these were essential to keep the car running. Mac pulled away and we overtook Murray who was walking briskly down the road. I slouched down in the back hoping he wouldn't see me.

"This your first operational squadron?" Mac shouted over the noise of the engine.

"Yes, Sir," I replied.

"Don't worry about all that Sir guff. Not while we're on the squadron anyway. The boys call me Mac."

"God knows why?" said Barker, "He's about as Scottish as a weekend in Margate."

"I'm very proud of my Celtic roots," protested Mac. "You know my Maiden Aunt was at the Battle of Bannockburn." Mac laughed loudly at his own joke. We passed one of the hangars and I plucked up courage to ask a question.

"Did the squadron go up this morning?"

"Yes. Bloody awful weather though. They tried to vector us into some blip on a radar screen, but we couldn't see anything. Doc had radiator trouble and started to overheat so he put down at Manston. We're stood-down till eleven hundred, but I can't see they'll be much going on today, not with this cloud." I looked to the sky and agreed, there was no break in the overcast gloom. Mac turned on to the airfield and across the concrete apron.

That short journey in the back of the Bentley was a huge boost to my self esteem. Five minutes before I'd stood on the kerb feeling ludicrous and wretched, now I'd been welcomed into the company of two senior pilots. For the first time I started to feel I was actually a member of the squadron.

We reached the Dispersal Hut where the Hurricanes sat being refuelled and re-armed. Mac helped me out of the car with my equipment.

airborne and fighting within two minutes. The ground crew had to have the aircraft ready, and as a pilot you had to be in the right state of mind.

The room emptied as aircraft and equipment needed to be checked. With no duty for me to carry out I watched from the window. I saw HB walk around the aircraft and return to the hut. He stuck his head round the doorway and spoke to the corporal.

"Parker, ring through to sector control and tell them we're standing-to."

"Yes sir." The corporal picked up the receiver and wound the magneto handle on the side of the telephone. HB turned to look at me.

"You OK lad?"

"Yes Sir," I replied.

"We're still two aircraft down, so I can't get you up for a bit." I nodded. The corporal spoke into the telephone.

"Hello, hello control. Panther Squadron stood-to." He replaced the handset and made a note of the time on the foolscap pad.

The refuelling bowser and ammunition lorries had moved away, the squadron aircraft sat pointing into the wind and ready for action. I helped take a few of the chairs outside where some of the pilots sat waiting. One or two paced around like expectant fathers and others lay on the damp ground.

At fourteen minutes past eleven the telephone in the hut rang. Everybody stopped what they were doing and turned to the corporal. He picked up the handset with his left hand and grabbed a pencil with his right. He scribbled down a note and sprang from the desk. Through the open door, he shouted to HB.

"Single Bandit spotted inbound over Harwich.

33

Vector zero four five, Angels eight. Scramble three aircraft!"

HB turned to Mac.

"Okay, scramble Yellow Section."

It only took a matter of seconds for Mac, Freddie and Doc to strap on their parachutes and clamber up into the cockpits of their Hurricanes. Almost simultaneously the three engines came to life and the aircraft were bouncing away from us down the runway. They became airborne and headed north in a long turning climb. Very quickly they disappeared in the low cloud base only to reappear some fifteen minutes later. In something of an anti-climax, sector control had ordered them to return to base. The three aircraft taxied back into position and were quickly refuelled by the waiting ground crew.

As scheduled the whole squadron took off at twelve fifteen and by the time they had returned a steady drizzle had started. I sat and watched the activity on the airfield. Aviation had always fascinated me, but as entertaining as it was to watch the different types of aircraft arriving and departing, frustration was growing inside me about the lack of flying I was doing. The day continued with routine patrols, refuelling and rearming. Eventually the squadron stood-down and the operations book recorded an uneventful day for 506.

Chapter 3
Airborne

The following day was much warmer, but a thick haze hung over the channel which hampered visibility and deterred enemy attacks on our shipping. Before breakfast I reported to the dispersal hut with the other pilots, but my name had still not been added to the roster.

I spent the morning and afternoon as I had done the day before watching and waiting. With so much time to think I started to question why Hardy-Burton had not allowed me to go up. Had he seen something in my logbook that disturbed him? Had the incident with the Station Warrant Officer been a bigger issue than I'd thought? I occupied myself studying maps of the sector area and reading a selection of operational manuals that were scattered around the crew room. My first experience of warfare was far more tedious than I'd imagined.

The squadron had patrolled twice before midday and in the afternoon was scrambled to intercept an attack on Dover. When they returned late in the afternoon, there was an element of excitement as Green Section, led by Warwick, had run into a scrap with two Messerschmitt 109 fighters. Both Warwick and Long had managed to score hits on one of the fighters while Cavendish took the other head on. He'd seen puffs of black smoke coming from the German's engine and claimed a probable kill. However, his own aircraft had taken substantial damage, but he'd managed to limp back to North Weald with reduced engine power.

I was sitting outside the crew room, staring at the clouds and deep in a mediocre daydream when someone called my name. I shot up from the chair, it was HB.

"Grab your gear. You're coming up with me in five minutes." He looked over towards the airfield and pointed at one of the Hurricanes. "Take Aussie's kite."

"Yes sir." I dived into the hut and found a spare life jacket and parachute. As I ran out Aussie grabbed my arm and stopped me.

"Hey! You be careful." He nodded towards the Hurricane I was running for. "I've got very fond of her." He smiled, but there was a stern threat in his words.

It seemed odd to be so protective over a piece of machinery, but later I would understand just how strong a pilot's attachment to his aircraft could be.

I looked over the Hurricane trying to remember all the checks I was supposed to carry out before flying. I pulled and prodded a few things in an effort to look like I knew what I was doing. I was checking the gun bay covers had been properly fastened down when HB walked over. He was holding one of the maps I'd been studying in the crew room. He laid it on the wing next to me and produced a thick pencil from his pocket.

"We'll go up for twenty minutes or so," he said. "I'll lead and we'll make for eight thousand feet. Now I want you to get to know this area like the back of your hand." He drew a large circle around the south-east corner of Essex. "The biggest landmark south of here is the Thames, but don't get it confused with other stretches of water, like the Orwell and Blackwater up here. They're much smaller but in bad visibly they can look the same." He then stabbed his finger at

36

position.

"Back off a little. Give yourself space to look around." HB's voice came over the radio again. I eased back slightly and widened the gap between us. We had held the formation for some time when I saw him look over towards me.

"Good. Now I want you to form up directly behind me, on my tail at about fifty feet." He continued flying straight and level while I fell back slightly and slipped in behind him.

"In position skipper," I reported.

"Good. I'm going to break to port and I want you to keep on my tail. Understood?"

"Understood," I replied. We flew on and then suddenly he rolled his aircraft and dived. I moved the stick sharply to the left and pulled back. The world spun around in a blur. I still had sight of him, although he was now at a greater distance and diving. I chased him down. He pulled up hard and into a tight right hand turn. I kept with him. The turn became tighter and tighter. I was amazed that the aircraft could take such pressure as the G force pushed me hard into the seat. Then, just as I thought I was catching him he rolled again and dived. This time I lost sight of him. I scanned the sky. Where had he gone? Then, there he was, closing in on me directly ahead. I rolled to port and headed into another tight turn. In the mirror above my head I saw him looming down on me from behind. The situation had been reversed, he was now chasing me. I pulled back and climbed. As I did the aircraft lost speed and began to stall. I rolled slightly and nosed over to pick up speed. The radio crackled.

"Okay, good stuff. Let's call it off now." I looked in my mirror and sighed, despite my attempts to evade him he was still sitting about fifty feet off of my tail. I levelled off.

"Understood skipper."

"Hold your position. I'm going to join you on your starboard side. Now lead us home."

"Yes Skipper."

In all my training I'd never led a formation, even though there were only two aircraft the task was quite daunting. I now had to navigate and find a route home. It takes very little to become disorientated in combat. In our aerial horse play, which had lasted only moments, we'd lost six thousand feet and were heading dead south, somewhere over Southern England. I looked around and managed to identify the town of Romford below us and from there it was easy to find the airfield. Fortunately, it was a crystal clear evening, but in thick cloud or low light it would have been a different matter. We turned north and descended into the circuit. By then the setting sun was casting long shadows on the ground and tinting the clouds pink. We touched down on the grass and taxied towards the waiting ground crew. I cut the engine and removed my helmet. My hair was soaked with sweat. Edwards jumped up on the wing and appeared over the cockpit wall.

"Back in one piece. That's a good start."

With our parachutes over our shoulders HB and I walked back to the Dispersal Hut.

"Good show," he said. "You did well to stay on me, but if you're a spot like that again don't climb and stall. You gave me a clean shot at the end. Best bet is to push the nose over, use all the speed you've got and turn tight. These old kites will out turn most Jerry fighters." He pointed back at the aircraft. "Remember

A few early mourners had gathered between the grey lichen covered gravestones. At the porch we were met by the verger.

"I'm terribly sorry, the bellows have been punctured and we got no organ. So I'm afraid it's only the piano today." He handed us two small hymn books. We sat uncomfortably on the hard pew as the nave filled with people. For fear of catching someone's eye, I avoided looking at the congregation and stared at the sunlight streaming through a stained glass image of Simeon holding an infant Jesus.

An elderly vicar appeared from the narrow vestry door. He greeted us with a voice that sounded far stronger than his frail frame suggested it should be. He asked us to stand and a hundred black clad figures rose in silence. From the choir stalls the opening bars of an obscure piece by Bach resonated from an antique piano. I had never attended a funeral before and was unsure of what expression I should wear on my face. There came a shuffling of feet and I turned to see Warrant Officer Murray marching a perfect military step down the aisle. In front of him was the coffin, covered with a Union Jack and carried on the shoulders of six non-commissioned ranks. In the small church with its white walls the cortege looked almost supernatural and I felt a chill run down my spine.

I learnt a fair bit about Ashley-Brown in that short service. How he'd excelled at school and captained the first fifteen. What his ambitions had been when he entered Queen's College Oxford. His courage and patriotism that led him to join up and how his life had been cut short. While a cousin gave a reading from the Book of John, I found myself staring at a woman. I assumed she was Ashley-Brown's wife.

She wore a smart black two-piece suit. I was captivated by her figure and profile which hid under a mesh veil. For me the prospect of meeting and marrying such an attractive woman seemed so remote.

At the graveside, as Ashley-Brown was being lowered into the ground, I stared at the coffin and tried to picture the man I'd never met. I kept thinking about the Hurricane I'd witnessed smashing into the ground just a few days before. That dreadful sound and the blinding flash from the explosion. Etched in my mind was a vision of the pilot as he battled with the controls. I realised then, I must have been the last person to see him alive.

The formalities ended and a grunt from Cavendish prompted me to leave.

"I'm going to send a telegram from the Post Office," he said as we pulled away from the verge. We drove at speed down the Epping Road, the wind whipping around the windscreen and ruffling the hair on the back of my head.

"It's a wonderful car." I tried again to make conversation, but all I got in return was a quick nod of the head. I didn't know if Cavendish was simply arrogant or the battle was taking such a toll on him he chose to be unsociable. Either way, being in his presence was uncomfortable.

In the village he parked on some cobbles outside a bakery and told me to wait with the car. I did as I was told. The wide market street was quiet with most of the businesses shut for lunch. I heard the bell on the bakery door tinkle as it opened and the baker in a well-worn set of whites came out. He walked around to my side of the car carrying a parcel wrapped in newspaper.

"Hello there," he said nervously. "You know we're all so grateful for what you chaps are doing." He thrust the parcel towards me. "It's not much, but please have these."

I was awash with embarrassment.

"Thank you." I took the parcel.

"Iced buns. My own recipe." I unwrapped the newspaper and the delicious aroma of the freshly baked pastry caught my nose. I shook his hand and told him I'd take them back to the squadron. He walked back to the shop and I noticed a young girl and boy watching from the window. I felt a complete fraud. At present my sole contribution to the war effort was a twenty minute proving flight. I wrapped the parcel up and slid it into the footwell under my legs so Cavendish didn't see. He appeared about five minutes later briskly walking along the pavement.

We drove back up the Epping Road and turned down towards the airfield. There was an almighty roar as six Hurricanes crossed overhead at low level. The purr of the finely tuned MG was drowned out by the Merlin engines. It was A-flight taking off for the afternoon patrol. I watched them climb into the blue sky and marvelled at how formidable they looked.

Back at the Dispersal I managed to smuggle the buns out of the car without Cavendish noticing and left them on a table in the crew room. Here I had no doubt they'd be consumed without enquiry. I'd just found a seat in the sunshine when the Adjutant called me from an open window.

"Trot on over to Hangar two will you," he said. "There's a Hurricane that's just arrived from Brooklands. It needs a flight test before it's put on to squadron strength."

He leaned further out of the window and pointed to the other side of the airfield where I could just see the distinctive tailplane and fin flash. "Edwards will take you over. When you've finished park her up here."

"Yes sir." I'd never performed a flight test before. Although a little nervous at the thought I was buoyed by the chance of getting airborne again.

I found Flight Sergeant Edwards with two fitters who'd just demolished the iced buns. I was glad they'd found a good home.

"So what were you doing before all this then?" he asked me as we walked over to the hangar.

"I was just about to finish my apprenticeship at Armstrong Whitworth."

"On the shop floor?"

"No, drawing office."

"That's what my boy wants to do. He's good at his maths, but whether they'll take him I don't know."

As we ambled over in the afternoon sunshine he spoke a lot about his family. He was a genuine cockney, born off Bromley High Street well within the sound of Bow Bells.

On the concrete apron in front of Hangar Two was Hawker Hurricane V5667; it was brand new and unblemished by action. Edwards stopped and cocked his head to one side.

"Now first thing I do when checking over an aircraft is look at it from a distance." He folded his arms.

"You see if she's rigged wrong, tyres soft or one of the oleo's leaking, you might not spot it from up close." He studied the aircraft and I felt compelled to do the same. When he seemed satisfied we walked over to it. I slung my parachute on the tailplane and we continued the inspection.

Underneath the engine cowling he stooped down and ran his finger through a small pool of fluid on the concrete.

"All aircraft mark their territory with a bit of oil." He studied the fluid on his finger. "We can cope with that, but what you've got to look out for is water or glycol. The last thing you want is a split hose or punctured radiator. She looks ok."

We spent the next fifteen minutes wiggling pipes, tightening screws and checking fluids until Edwards was happy. I could see why he was popular among the pilots, he had such confidence in his engineering abilities that made you feel nothing could go wrong with an aircraft he was looking after.

He helped me don my parachute and I clambered into the cockpit. As he stood on the wing I looked up at his narrow face with the bright sunshine behind him.

"It's not for me to tell you what to do up there, but I'd take it easy. Give yourself plenty of altitude, try a few gentle turns before you throw her around." He went to jump down, but turned back. "Oh and I'd double check those controls are dead right. I've known these come out of the factories with the cables round the wrong way."

I raised the seat up to a comfortable position. To the front was the instrument panel, under which my legs stretched out either side of the control column. I took a moment to get comfortable in the seat and then slid my hands into the thin leather flying gloves and plugged in my headset.

Directly in front of me was the twelve cylinder Merlin engine, patiently waiting for ignition. With the aid of a slip of paper I ran through the pre-flight checks. Fuel, all three tanks full, one hundred and five gallons in total. I moved the control column forwards, backwards and then side to side checking for full and free movement. The parking brake, which looked no bigger than one found on a push bike was on and locked. Radiator shutter open. With my left hand I pushed the throttle lever open by half an inch. Mixture control: full rich. I reached forward with my other hand and pumped the brass priming handle, spraying a fine mist of fuel into the air intake that would help the engine start from cold. Switch the magnetos on. The engine was now primed, and the ignition system was live. I looked out from the cockpit to check that no one was standing near the propeller. At the port wingtip was Edwards, he signalled it was all clear with a raised thumb. I drew breath and shouted.

'Contact!'

With my middle and index fingers I pushed the two black Bakelite buttons by my left knee. A whining came from under the engine cowling and the propeller jerked round a few degrees and stopped. I kept my fingers pressed on the buttons and it jerked again, this time producing a puff of white smoke from the exhaust stubs. A third movement and the engine started. The sudden noise rolled across the airfield and put up a flock of crows. Inside the cockpit it was hard to hear how the engine was running. I looked back at Edwards who was staring at the machine, looking to see if anything was leaking and listening to the pitch of the Merlin.

He smiled at me, it was running smoothly. With a wave of my hand I signalled for the chocks to be removed. Edwards edged towards the fuselage. The heavy propeller spinning rapidly just a few feet from his body pushed him against the wing. Collecting the chocks was a dangerous pursuit; a miss timed movement or a slip on the concrete could result in a lost limb or worse. Ducking under the wing he grabbed the rope that held the chocks together and moved quickly away. Now the two and a half ton fighter was being kept still by the brake lever at my fingertips. Holding the stick back against my stomach I pushed the throttle further forward and ran the engine up. I watched the oil pressure rise and then stabilise. Everything else looked good. I brought the engine back to idle. I checked the wind direction and looked above and behind for any other aircraft. I gently released the parking brake and the aircraft started to move. Edwards was watching with arms folded and his head cocked to one side again. I taxied parallel to the runway and when I judged I'd gone far enough applied a little left brake with my foot. I increased the throttle to bring the nose round. One final check of the sky above and I started to bump down the runway. The tail started to lift and I could see over the long nose cowling. The ground beneath me dropped away slightly and I was airborne. I quickly retracted the undercarriage and two red lights appeared on the position indicator.

Flying alone with no fixed agenda is a freedom like no other. The driver of a car or rider of a motorbike is governed by the direction of the road, a sailor is governed by the wind and tides, but the pilot can move freely within a three dimensional space.

Some might find this daunting, but for me it had felt natural ever since my first solo flight.

I decided to head north so turned to starboard all the while holding a steady climb. At five thousand feet little England looked peaceful. The hot summer had covered the countryside in rectangles of yellow and brown.

Heeding Edwards' advice I eased over into a lazy figure of eight turn and back the other way. Then a tighter turn, first to port, then to starboard. The machine felt good. I dropped the nose and then pulled back, bringing the aircraft up into a vertical climb and letting her fall backwards until I was inverted. Here I rolled off the top straight and level. I repeated the movement, but this time pulled back harder. I strained to look up as the ground appeared above my head. I followed through into a vertical dive and levelled off to complete a perfect three hundred and sixty degree loop. Next, I performed a wide barrel roll and then a quick snap roll.

It seemed bizarre, I was twenty one years old, flying one of the fastest machines in the world and enjoying myself at five thousand feet while below me Europe was at war.

I could find no fault in the aircraft and decided to head back to North Weald. I slowly descended through the summer haze. At a thousand feet I throttled back and opened the canopy. A welcome blast of air curled around the stuffy cockpit. Undercarriage down, the indicator showed two green lights. Five hundred feet, I lowered the flaps and slipped into the approach.

Down, down, bump. I throttled right back and let the aircraft start to slow on the grass runway. Then very slowly squeezed the brake lever. I taxied off the strip and towards the Dispersal Hut. A-flight had now returned from patrol so I parked neatly at the end of the line of aircraft. I energetically bounded out of the cockpit and gave my report on how she handled to

Edwards.

As I walked up to the Dispersal with my parachute I noticed the body language of the pilots was more animated than usual. A group of people were studying the tail plane of Freddie Fuller's Hurricane. The fabric had been badly ripped in places exposing the metal framework underneath. Mac, with his ruffled blonde hair and two red marks on his temple where his goggles had sat, was talking to the intelligence officers. He was gesturing with his hands and demonstrating some form of aerobatic manoeuvre. Aussie stood next to him inhaling a great lungful of smoke from a rapidly shortening cigarette. Inside the crew room Warwick was pouring tea.

"Good show?" I asked enthusiastically.

"Hell of a scrap," he answered while his eyes concentrated on the boiling water cascading into an enamel mug.

"They steered us on to a swarm of Stukas that were beating up an oil tanker off Margate. The CO, and Doc got one a piece. Then their top cover, about 20 109s, dropped on us from above. Mac picked one off and Aussie got a probable." He placed the kettle back on the stove. "There'll be a party tonight! That gives Mac his five, so there's another Ace in the squadron." He gestured towards the mug. "Sorry did you want one?" I nodded and he picked the kettle up again.

"We lost Barker though." He said indifferently, as if he was letting me know the cricket score.

"Is he missing?" I asked rather naively.

"No, he hit the water vertically." Warwick stirred the tea slowly. "I don't think there would be much of him left."

The intelligence officers stayed for a while to

garner as much information as they could and then raced off in their staff car.

"How was the flight test?" I looked around to see Hardy-Burton standing beside me.

"Good Sir, no problems," I answered. "I took her up to five thousand, she seemed to be fine."

"Okay, you'll be on the roster tomorrow morning." He walked off to his office where the Adjutant was waiting with yet another pile of papers.

Chapter 5
Your round

I was anxious about flying with the squadron at dawn so decided on an early night. After dinner in the Sergeant's Mess I sat in an anteroom listening to the wireless. I was in time to catch the news. The headlines still suggested that Hitler was keen on invading us and more German troops were being moved towards the Channel ports. The way in which the situation was reported through the airwaves made it feel so far away. As if I was listening to events happening on the other side of the world and yet those troops were less than a hundred miles away from where I was sitting.

I heard the telephone ring behind the bar and the steward with his hand over the receiver asked if any 506 pilots were available. Being the only one in close proximity I took the call.

"Hello Sommers here."

"Sommers it's Aussie." came the voice down the other end. "We're heading to the Kings Head for a few drinks to celebrate Mac's fifth. You boys be outside in five minutes." The phone clicked and he rang off. It felt much more like an order than a social invitation.

In the early part of the Great War a French newspaper had declared Adolphe Pégoud as Le Ace because he had managed to shoot down five enemy aircraft. This unofficial term was recognised as great propaganda by the Allied High Command and from then on it was widely regarded that any pilot who achieved more than five confirmed kills was considered an Ace.

The tradition had continued and within the RAF there was always a celebration when a pilot earned this distinction. HB had already shot down six aircraft, so now along with Mac there were two aces in 506.

Five minutes later I stood on the steps of the mess with Freddie, Lanky and Hill. A tiny bright red Austin Seven came careering round the corner. Aussie was in the driving seat grinning madly while Doc sat in the passenger seat clinging to the dashboard. Following behind and dwarfing the little Austin was Mac in the Bentley. They both skidded to a halt at the bottom of the steps.

It was a tight squeeze getting all nine pilots into both cars. I ended up sitting on the spare wheel of the Bentley and gripping the hood frame. Much to Aussie's disapproval, Mac overtook the little Austin as soon as we left the Station gates. We led all the way down through the narrow lanes, and I prayed that the spare wheel was properly secured.

The King's Head was a typical coaching inn. Generations of landlords had left their mark by either adding or removing parts of the building which meant no wall was perpendicular and the roofline undulated in every direction. Above the oak door with its small square window the sign proclaimed that Mr Ivor Potts was the licensee. The public bar was a square room with an awkward corner. The low wooden beams were separated by strips of nicotine stained plaster. A large open fire dominated the room and a bar ran along the wall opposite, behind which an array of bottles collected dust on narrow shelves.

The walls were cluttered with pictures and ornaments. A Cromwellian breastplate and helmet were mounted above the fireplace. Next to a window a set of cutlasses crossed their blades below a duelling pistol. Faded etchings depicting the Battles of Barrosa, Waterloo and Salamanca hung unevenly on the old plaster. At the far end a dart board and oche was tucked into the corner.

We piled in and crowded the room, much to the bewilderment of the locals who were enjoying a quiet pint. Mr Potts was polishing a glass. He was a small man with a crop of white hair and yellow eyebrows. The rush of nine customers all appearing at the same time seemed to alarm him.

"It's Mac's celebration so he can buy the drinks," shouted Aussie.

"You can bugger off!" replied Mac. "Yes. It is my celebration. So you buy me a drink!"

"OK, just this once." Aussie relented. "But when I get my fifth, drinks are on you buddy!" He looked around and counted the blue uniforms.

"Ah what the hell! Nine pints of bitter."

Potts put down his cloth and set to work serving the drinks. Doc and Freddie moved towards the dart board where two young farmers were in the middle of a game. I picked up one of the freshly poured pints. The murky brown liquid matched the colour of the oak beams. Mac picked up another and offered me a cigarette, I accepted.

"You'll be my number two tomorrow," he said producing a silver lighter from his pocket.

As with most fighter squadrons, 506 was split into two flights A and B. Those flights were then split again into two sections, all of which contained three aircraft and were colour coded. In A-flight there was Blue and Green Section. In B-flight the sections were coded Yellow and Red. Each flight had its own leader as did each section. In this way the squadron could operate as one whole unit of twelve aircraft or be split into smaller units of six or three. Hardy-Burton commanded A-flight and Mac B-flight.

The flame from the lighter curled towards me as Mac lit my cigarette.

"You play any sports? Rugby?" he asked.

"I'm more of a cricket player," I answered and then proudly added. "I played a couple of times at county level."

"Ah even better." Mac exclaimed. "What's the mark of a good batsman?" I furrowed my brow at his question and he continued.

"A good batsman knows instinctively where every fielder is on the pitch. Almost like a sixth sense. He doesn't have to keep looking over his shoulder to see how the slips are arranged or where the square leg is, he just knows. He does this by not concentrating on just one fielder but by taking in the whole pitch. That means when the ball comes flying down the offside he can belt it into a safe area without thinking." Mac drew on his cigarette. "It's exactly the same up there. A good fighter pilot takes in the whole sky, not just the aircraft he's flying alongside or the one he's chasing down. You've got to develop your own sixth sense so if you suddenly break hard right you know exactly where that's going to put you in relation to the dogfight." I sipped my beer and listened as he went on.

"Do you know Boelcke's ten rules?" I nodded. Oswald Boelcke was a German fighter Ace. In 1916 he wrote the Dicta Boelcke which comprised the ten rules of air fighting. The rules were adopted by both the Germans and the Allies and were still the foundation of fighter pilot training almost twenty five years later. As a teenager I had read and memorised the Dicta before I'd applied for pilot training.

"Remember this." He poked me in the clavicle to ensure I was listening. "The two most important of those rules are, never run away if you get attacked, turn and fight, and don't fire until you're in close range. I've seen so many pilots waste their chances and all their ammunition taking pot shots at an aircraft from twelve hundred feet."

"You're not talking shop I hope." Warwick pushed his way between us to pick up a pint. "Is he giving you Mac's code of dogfighting etiquette?" I gave a nervous guffaw. Warwick rocked back on his heels and puffed on his pipe.

"The rules of engagement are so." He said mimicking Mac. "One - never talk about politics or money in the mess. Two - never talk about work in the pub." Aussie appeared with an empty glass and slammed it down on the bar.

"Three - always make sure you can get out of the window in case her husband comes home early." There was a roar of laughter.

I learnt a lot about Mac and the other pilots that night. Mac and Warwick were regular officers who'd joined up in 1937. Warwick was the oldest in the squadron. He came from a family of bankers and to avoid the prospect of a dull career in the city had hidden away in the Air Force.

Mac was the son of a surgeon. He was married and had a son who'd been born just before the squadron had been posted to France earlier in the year

Aussie had been commissioned in the Australian infantry and spent two years flying for the Queensland Mining Company. He'd fallen in love with a cabaret singer whom he'd followed to London in the summer of 1939. However, she spurned his offer of marriage and he was left unemployed and homeless. An uncle in the Australian embassy happened to have connections in Whitehall and by pulling various strings managed to get Aussie a commission in the Royal Air Force.

By ten o'clock the darts match reached a tense climax in which the Essex Agricultural Workers Union beat the Royal Air Force by a narrow margin. We finished our drinks and piled out into the balmy evening with the prospect of a very early morning.

Chapter 6
Waking in the dark

I was in a deep comfortable slumber when a large violent hand shook me awake. It took a lot of effort to prise my eyes apart. The duty corporal was towering over me.

"Morning Sarge, tea and toast downstairs." My wristwatch said four o'clock.

"Do you mind signing here." The corporal opened the daybook which proved he had carried out his orders and I had been roused for duty.

I passed on the tea and toast, early mornings often made me feel nauseous. Outside we bundled into the back of the same Bedford lorry which I'd arrived in. It was pitch black under the canvas cover. Freddie lit a cigarette and for a brief second our faces were illuminated like a renaissance painting.

At the Dispersal Hut there was more tea and cigarettes. A few songbirds were leading the dawn chorus and a very thin sliver of orange light silhouetted the eastern horizon. No wonder Roman soldiers worshiped Aurora, goddess of the dawn. Even in wartime there was a magical optimism about this time of day. I saw HB check his watch.

"Fifteen minutes everybody."

By the time we were airborne it was first light. In the lead aircraft HB waited until we had formed up behind him. Then I heard the radio hum and he spoke.

"Catnap control, this is Panther leader. Panther Squadron airborne." From somewhere below in a concrete bunker a voice crackled back.

"Panther Leader, this is Catnap control. Vector one

eight zero."

Panther was our squadron codename and Catnap was the name for our sector control. Under the Dowding Air Defence System the entire country had been divided up into groups and sectors. When a raid was detected the controllers would then direct available fighters to intercept the enemy. The Catnap controller on duty that day was a former pilot himself. He had a slow purposeful voice which emanated from the very bottom of his chest and was affectionately nicknamed Aunty.

"Vector one eight zero, understood." HB acknowledged the instruction. He then signalled to us that he was going to turn. His port wing dropped and banked, the squadron followed moving together as one unit. The compass in my cockpit rotated through the degrees until it read one hundred and eighty, due south. I held my position to the starboard quarter of Mac's aircraft.

We flew on for a good thirty miles. Over the town of Sevenoaks we gently turned back north and flew the route we'd just taken in reverse. We were to repeat this pattern over the east of London and the Thames Estuary until we spotted any enemy aircraft or the sector control gave us other orders.

Above Dartford I looked out from the cockpit. Cranes and chimneys flanked the river and clusters of barrage balloons were dotted around. These large balloons were filled with enough hydrogen to carry a thick wire cable to five thousand feet. The network of balloons and wire formed a barrier to stop any low flying aircraft.

They floated tethered and motionless like a shoal of silver jelly fish with their deadly tentacles trailing below. Across to the east the estuary widened and reached out to the sea. An array of different ships were steaming to and fro. Battleships, cargo ships and tankers. A few barges were under sail and making good use of the prevailing wind.

The radio hummed, Aunty spoke again.

"Panther Squadron, this is Catnap. Vector one one zero and make angels eleven."

I interpreted the instruction in my head: turn southeast and climb to eleven thousand feet.

Still holding formation we crossed the estuary and gained height.

As the altitude increased the air pressure dropped and it became colder inside my cockpit. My flying jacket, now dry but still stiff, became an essential piece of equipment. Beyond ten thousand feet I breathed the oxygen fed to me via my mask. From this altitude it was possible to see the entire county of Kent. The garden of England, lush and green, bordered by the wriggling coastline.

The radio hummed once more.

"Panther this is Catnap. I have some trade for you. Bandits now ten miles east of Ramsgate." The direction we were heading on would take us straight over Ramsgate so we held the course.

"Keep your eyes peeled everyone." HB warned us.

The sky was clear and in the distance I could see the English channel sparkling beyond. I found it hard to concentrate on keeping formation and at the same time scanning the sky for enemy aircraft.

It didn't help that we were flying directly towards the bright morning sun which hindered our vision. Through the canopy I noticed five or six tiny black dots. I watched them for a moment trying to workout if they were aircraft, birds or just marks on the Perspex. The radio hummed and this time Aussie's voice came through.

"Bandits! One o'clock low skipper."

"Yeah, I've got them too," said another pilot.

"They're low. Stukas I reckon."

"Okay, I see 'em." HB's voice of authority cut through the chitchat. "B-flight hold top cover. A-flight on me..... Tally Ho!"

With that the six aircraft of A-flight broke to the left and started to dive towards the black dots which had now become clearer in my vision. From above I watched HB bring his flight around in a sweeping turn to start the attack.

"Bandits two o'clock!" The sharp shout over the radio startled me. I looked right to see another four aircraft about two thousand feet away and heading straight for us. They must have been the fighter escorts for the bombers.

"Take them straight on." I heard Mac say and he turned sharply to starboard. This caught me out and I had to turn hard to avoid hitting him. I lost speed and by the time I'd corrected myself I'd dropped away from the formation. We were now head on with the four fighters. I flicked on the gunsight and twisted the brass ring on the gun button to make my weapons live.

The bright sun turned the oncoming fighters into jet black silhouettes. Squinting through the sight I selected the aircraft on the far right, but then I noticed the one alongside was converging on a better trajectory. I pulled over slightly to re aim, but I was forced to correct my position which cost me valuable time. I snarled in anger at my stupidity for changing targets. My aim was now hopelessly out, but in pure frustration I pressed the gun button anyway. I felt the control column judder as the eight browning machine guns chattered into life. The four fighters passed over me in a blur and my bullets headed harmless off towards the English Channel.

As soon as they passed I dropped my port wing and turned as tight as I could to face them again. They were now heading away from me and I was already a thousand feet to their rear. In an effort to catch them I rammed the throttle lever forward and pulled the booster control toggle open. I now had a clear view of the four aircraft. They were Messerschmitt 109s, smaller and more compact than our Hurricanes. Their engine cowlings were a brilliant yellow which stood out against the grey cloud. The top of the wings had a jagged two-tone grey camouflage which looked like an abstract artwork.

Try as I may, I was unable to catch my quarry and the distance between us grew greater. They flew in a descending spiral bringing them into the dogfight which had developed between the Stukas and the other Hurricanes.

The 109 on the inside of the formation began to turn in towards the fight. I pushed forward and dropped my nose into an almost vertical dive, hoping to pounce on him from above.

The sudden movement briefly starved my engine of fuel and it misfired, but I dived down wildly with complete disregard for my engine or aircraft. My speed was now excessive and the controls had become heavy. The little German fighter broke to the right. With the speed I was carrying I was unable to turn with him. I pulled back on the stick and for the briefest of moments he crossed in front of my gun sight. I tried a second burst from my guns, but the range was far too great to do any damage. I throttled back and slammed the booster control shut.

In what could have been no more than a few seconds I had become completely disoriented and lost sight of Mac. Uncertain of what to do I banked to the side and looked down. I caught sight of a Hurricane that was locked on the tail of a Stuka. The lumbering bomber was pumping out black smoke as he tried to run for the channel. The other raiders had disappeared. A heavily listing ship and columns of smoke rising from Ramsgate Harbour below suggested we had been too late to stop the raid.

The radio had been buzzing in my ears, but with all the confusion I'd not been listening to what was being said. I suddenly heard my own call sign.

"Yellow two, I'm coming up behind you." I looked up into the mirror and saw Mac approaching from the rear. I throttled back to let him overtake and then formed up in my position off of his starboard quarter. We circled the area for a while.

"Looks like the show's over," he remarked. "Let's head back."

A quarter of an hour later we were landing at North Weald. Two aircraft had already made it back and a further three were following us in.

I taxied up to the Dispersal Hut and spun round into wind. Edwards appeared out of nowhere and jumped on the wing. As I cut the engine he lent into the cockpit and pushed my hand away from the control column. His grubby fingers clicked the gun button to safe. I feel such a fool, I'd flown in and landed with my weapons live.

"Sorry about that," I murmured sheepishly.

"You're not the first." He looked at me with a knowing grin. "It's always the first thing I check."

After that I diligently went through the post flight checks, turned off the battery and ensured the fuel cocks were closed. I undid my straps and went to pull myself out of the seat. As I stood up I became aware of pain on the outside of my left leg. I'd been so tense that my knee had been rubbing against the tubular airframe and I'd given myself a friction burn. A stupid injury but bloody painful.

I joined Mac outside the Dispersal Hut where he offered me a cigarette. The morning sun was warm and I was still wearing my jacket, but I was suddenly overcome with a cold shiver. As I lifted my hand I noticed I was shaking. The excitement of the dogfight had sent me into a state of mild shock.

"You okay?" Mac looked at me.

"Yes. I'm fine," I replied inhaling a lung full of tobacco. The smoke spread through my chest cavity and my nerves calmed.

"I lost sight of you after we took the 109s head on," he said. "Did you manage to have a crack at one?"

"Only from a distance. Don't think I hit anything."

"Make sure you keep moving around and keep a good lookout. When I spotted you, you were cruising straight and level. You didn't see me till I called you. If I'd been a Jerry you'd never have stood a chance."

I acknowledged the gentle reprimand with a solemn nod of the head.

As they always did, the intelligence officers had arrived with their notepads. One of them, an officer by the name of Shelton, approached me.

"Were you flying this morning?" he enquired.

"Yes sir."

"Did you engage the enemy?" I thought for a moment.

"Yes, well I tried to." I went to recount what had just happened.

"What were the markings on the Messerschmitt you saw?" he asked.

"Markings? Eh… they were painted in grey camouflage?"

"Yes, did they have any distinctive markings?" He lowered his notepad like a disappointed school teacher. "Did they have any squadron emblems? Numbers on the fuselage? Were the wing tips yellow or another colour?"

I thought hard, but in my mind it was all such a blur. I could picture the aircraft, jet black in silhouette but beyond that could remember little else. He sighed and moved on to question Doc and Aussie who had just landed.

HB arrived and appeared pleased with our efforts. Aussie had bagged his second Stuka and Warwick had had to put down at Hornchurch. He had taken a volley of return fire from another Stuka and had found his rudder was badly damaged.

The erks had made short work of refuelling and re-arming the aircraft and within thirty minutes we were back at a state of readiness. I'd begun to feel hungry and needed refuelling myself. I was about to set off on a hunt for sustenance when I heard the crew room telephone ring. We all stood still and silent watching the corporal. He picked up the receiver then leapt from the chair and shouted through the door.

"Raid in bound. Squadron scramble!"

The reaction was instantaneous. All twelve pilots turned and ran for their aircraft. Mugs were dropped on the grass, once again magazines and newspapers discarded and chairs upended as we pushed past each other. My parachute was where I'd left it on the tailplane of my Hurricane. The straps were in a pile and I had to untangle the canvas webbing. The aircraft all began to burst into life. My own engine was started by Edwards who saw I was struggling with my parachute. The wash of the propeller caught me and the canvas straps I'd been wrestling with flailed around in the air. Eventually I managed to catch them all and attach myself to the parachute. Edwards was out of the cockpit and waiting for me in his familiar stance on the wing. I'd only just got my legs in when I noticed other aircraft starting to move. By the time I'd strapped and plugged in they were starting to get airborne. I released the parking brake as Edwards jumped clear and I trundled down the runway. I was the last aircraft airborne and had to negotiate flying through the rear of the formation to get into my position.

The radio hummed and I heard HB's voice.

"Catnap, Panther leader. Panther airborne." There was a pause before Aunty at sector control answered.

"Panther Leader vector one seven zero. Make angels ten."

We flew on for three minutes or so then sector control called again.

"Panther Leader vector one five five. Bandits now at angels eight." The squadron turned gently onto the new course heading towards Canvey Island. I peered through the wispy cloud looking for any sign of the enemy. As we reached seven thousand feet Aunty called again.

"Panther Leader, false alarm, return home."

"For God's sake Aunty, make up your bloody mind!" came HB's reply. It was the first time I heard him get angry.

"Okay everyone, on me we're heading home."

In my haste to get airborne I twisted the straps on my parachute and the canvas was now digging into my left leg. I twisted and squirmed in an effort to get comfortable, all the while trying to maintain my position. The soreness on my knee added to the discomfort. I was glad to touch down and release the straps. I was even happier when I spotted lunch had arrived. Having not eaten since the previous day I was ravenous. Before eating I laid my parachute out neatly across the tailplane, this time with the straps untangled. My first two operational sorties had been tougher than I imagined. I walked back to the hut in a melancholic mood wondering if I was really cut out to be a fighter pilot.

I found my old deck chair and relaxed with a cheddar cheese sandwich in one hand and a cup of coffee in the other. Mabel casually sniffed her way over to me and sat down at my feet.

She widened her dark eyes and looked mournfully at my sandwich with an expression that any street urchin would have been proud of. It was less than a minute before I caved and threw her a crust.

Doc sat alongside me. With pencil in hand he was attacking the Times crossword. Aussie lay on the grass in front of us with his flying jacket folded under his head.

"'An optical projector?" muttered Doc. "Eleven letters E blank blank D?"

"I can't see what you get out of doing those damn puzzles." Aussie moaned from the ground.

"They stimulate the brain and relieve the boredom." Doc's eyes were still fixed on the page.

"The last thing I wanna do is stimulate my brain." said Aussie "What were you doing before the war kicked off?"

"Medical school. Second year at Edinburgh."

"Figures out. I had you down as a brainy kid."

"On the contrary, I was just about to fail. So Adolf's little foray into Poland couldn't have come at a better time."

"Epidiascope?" I blurted out, as the answer to the crossword clue popped into my brain. Doc looked back at the paper.

"Yes, that makes four down Canopus."

Cavendish strode over towards us. He was wearing a smart olive green flying suit with a fur lined collar.

"I take it you were flying G - George this morning Delaney."

Each aircraft was painted with three large white letters. The first two letters signified which squadron the aircraft was assigned to. The last letter was individual to that particular aircraft.

Doc looked up and squinted at Cavendish who stood with his back to the sun.

"Yes, G George." he confirmed. Cavendish flared his nostrils.

"Next time you're in a dogfight keep your bloody eyes open," He ranted. "I had a clean shot on that Stuka until you decided to try and bounce him. Do it again and I'll open up on you!"

Doc sat silent. Having made his point Cavendish walked away to harass a group of erks who were working on his aircraft.

"Honestly, that guy's a pain in the neck." Doc

hissed under his breath.

"Careful." said Aussie who was staring at the clouds. "Don't go bad mouthing a superior officer." He paused for a moment. "The guy may be an ass, but he's had his fair share of trouble."

I chewed on the sandwich and sipped my coffee as the ground crew finished preparing the aircraft. The excitement and shock of being scrambled earlier had a profound effect on me. As the hose was withdrawn from the last Hurricane to be refuelled and the armourers tightened up the fasteners on the gun panels I felt a small knot form in the pit of my stomach. The aircraft were now ready and we could at any moment be ordered into the air. I looked over to the crew room where I could see the corporal waiting by the telephone.

An anxiety started to spread from my stomach and I began to feel restless. It would be six weeks before that feeling left me.

We weren't scrambled that afternoon, but B-flight was scheduled to patrol at thirteen hundred.

Just as before, we flew a wide zig zag over the Thames estuary. By then the cloud base had lowered and beads of moisture streaked down the sides of my canopy.

"Four bandits due west, very low," said one of the pilots from the Red Section who were immediately behind us. As I was on the starboard side of the formation my view was obstructed by the other aircraft.

"Okay, I've got them," came Mac's reply. He gave a gentle waggle on his wings and we started to descend. After losing about two thousand feet we made a wide turn to port. This brought us to their rear with the sun behind us. I saw them, a thousand feet below and outlined against the green grey water. Four Messerschmitt 110 bombers.

"Tally Ho! B-flight," Mac called over the radio. It was the signal for us to begin the attack. I turned on the gunsight and the orange cross hair appeared on the four inch wide piece of glass. I checked my speed. We were gaining on them quite quickly so I throttled back. Then I picked the last aircraft on the starboard side as my target, this time I was going to stay with him. The sun shimmered on the canopies of the German bombers as they sped towards the mouth of the River Medway.

The 110 was a twin-engine aircraft with the speed of a fighter and the power of a bomber. It was reasonably fast and well armed, but not as agile as a Hurricane. The pilot sat forward between the two Daimler-Benz engines and behind him, facing rearward, was the gunner equipped with a seven point nine two millimetre machine gun.

Out of the corner of my eye I noticed another Hurricane converging on a similar attack. I tried to relax, but my left leg was tense again and my knee pushed against the frame. I was about fifteen hundred feet away.

"Hold your fire." I muttered to myself. Twelve hundred feet. A thousand feet. Eight hundred feet. "Hold your fire." My attack was textbook, I was now dead level and at a range of six hundred feet. Then I noticed a small bright orange blur come from the rear of the bomber. I thought at first it was a flare, but it was followed by several others in close succession. These small, harmless looking luminous blobs were in fact machine gun tracers. Stupidly I wondered who they were firing at and then realised it was me.

Now the distance was four hundred feet and just as I went to fire the 110 pulled hard to starboard. I turned to follow him and he crossed in front of my sight. I quickly pressed the gun button, rattling off a short burst towards him. As I did so the control column juddered and I assumed I'd hit some turbulent air. Another Hurricane swooped past and followed up my attack. I'd lost speed in the turn so dropped the nose slightly and opened the throttle. I continued round until I could fall in behind the other Hurricane which was still firing on the 110.

I watched his bullets rip through the wing. I noticed the machine gun had stopped firing and I could see the slumped figure of a man in the rear cockpit. Smoke started to cascade from the port engine and then suddenly the propeller separated. As it did the aircraft immediately rolled onto its back and plummeted down.

We were now only about five hundred feet high. The 110 pitched into waves spraying up a mass of water.

It was Doc in the other Hurricane who'd just sent the two German crew to the bottom of Davy Jones' locker.

Mac was pleased to report our efforts to Shelton when we arrived back. Out of the four 110s we'd intercepted, we had destroyed two. I had even managed to improve my observational skills and described the combat in far greater detail than I'd managed earlier that day.

After the debriefing Edwards approached me.

"I take it you had a bit of a scrap up there today?" he questioned. "I think you'd better come and have a look at this." He nodded his head towards my Hurricane. We walked over and from his pocket he pulled a long screwdriver. He crouched down under the port wing and I followed him.

"Now then, I've just spotted this." He pushed the screwdriver into a jagged hole in the thin skin. There was another about six inches away.

"Looks like they got you."

I thought hard and then remembered the jolt I'd felt in the middle of the dogfight.

"That must have been the rear gunner," I said, staring at the freshly made aperture.

"Well you're lucky, half an inch to the right and he'd have had your control cables."

That evening I found myself climbing into bed earlier than I usually did. Seventeen hours had passed since dawn, it felt more like a month.

Until that day I'd only ever seen German aircraft in newsreels and photographs. Now the 109s screaming overhead and the 110 smashing into the sea were clear visions in my mind. I couldn't help thinking about the two bullet holes in my wing. Doc must have pumped hundreds of rounds of ammunition into that 110 before it crashed into the sea. They'd only hit me twice, but were half an inch from sending me to a similar place. I found myself starting to explore the concept of fate and destiny, but I quickly stopped that train of thought. Those were not good subjects for a fighter pilot.

Chapter 7
Boundary Six

If being woken before sunrise on the first morning was hard, the second morning was hellish. The duty corporal seemed overly cheerful for that time of day and I started to wonder if he was slightly sadistic. Lanky was tucking his shirt into his trousers, he looked at me as I fought my way out from under the blankets.

"Second morning of ops is always the worst," he remarked buttoning up his fly.

Judging on how I'd felt the morning before, I decided fighting on an empty stomach was not sensible, so I nibbled half a slice of toast before getting into the back of the lorry with the others. As we headed out towards the airfield Freddie shifted his posture and let out an enormous fart.

"Jesus Christ Man!" exclaimed Lanky. "Give us some bloody warning."

"It's those egg sandwiches from the NAAFI wagon."

"Whatever you do, don't light a match in here," warned Lanky. This reduced us to fits of laughter. The joke was puerile, but it was a great release of tension and as a result we arrived at the Dispersal Hut in good humour.

As the sun rose we flew an uneventful patrol down towards Kent and returned an hour and a half later. The weather was dull, although the clouds occasionally let the sunshine through.

While we sat outside the hut waiting for orders, Mac produced a cricket bat and ball from the rear seat of his Bentley.

"Let's see what your fielding skills are like then." He lobbed the ball towards Warwick who caught it safely with his pipe clenched between his teeth. Doc appeared from the crew room with an old tea chest that had been used to store firewood. Using this as a set of wickets we created a makeshift cricket pitch. Mac was first into bat. Warwick took up position as keeper, myself as mid-wicket and Lanky as cover. Doc started with a gentle underarm bowl which Mac drove straight back towards him.

After a few of these docile deliveries Lanky took up the bowling. With his height he had a fast pace and bowled a full pitch. Mac had no choice but to defend the shot. The next ball came down the leg side. This time Mac lashed out, catching the ball on the edge of the bat. It spun upwards and started to descend about eight feet from my position. I threw my body sideways and caught the ball one handed in mid-air.

"Good show!" shouted Warwick, and a ripple of applause followed from the onlookers.

"Right, my turn." Warwick grabbed the bat from Mac and took up the crease. Doc pitched a gentle overarm down the offside. Warwick lunged forward and belted it. The ball flew over our heads and with an almighty crash sailed straight through one of the crew room windows. The duty corporal almost fell back off his chair as he ducked to avoid the shower of glass.

"Four!" shouted Mac.

"Balls!" retorted Warwick. "That's a six if ever I saw one."

The Adjutant came out of the door to see what the commotion was.

"I'm putting that on your mess bill."

We moved the pitch away from the hut and agreed on playing defensive shots only. It felt good to be physically active, rather than just sitting and waiting for the next set of orders.

Over the next few days we had no enemy engagements, which gave me valuable time to hone my flying skills and learn the geography of the area.

I was surprised at how quickly I became accustomed to the routine of rising in the dark and seeing the day break. I actually found myself starting to wake before the corporal had a chance to shake me. Strangely though Lanky was always awake before me and half dressed.

One morning we were told to assemble in the crew room. We'd not long returned from another unremarkable first light patrol. A Group Captain from somewhere up the chain of command had dropped by to issue orders and keep us on our toes. He gave us a few words of encouragement, stressed the importance of good team spirit and then left in a black staff car. As we pondered the reason for his visit, HB took the opportunity to speak to us.

"Most of our aircraft need maintenance, so we've been stood-down for the rest of the day."

"That means an afternoon off then sir?" asked Aussie optimistically.

"Unfortunately not." There were a couple of over dramatised sighs.

"I want you to take the time to calibrate your guns," HB continued. "I know the official recommendation is that guns are set to converge at twelve hundred feet, but I feel that's too far. In fact other squadrons are reporting better results with reducing that range."

The Browning machine guns that were fitted in the

wings of our Hurricanes were installed at a slight angle, which meant when fired the ammunition would converge at a given distance. This gave a concentrated spread of bullets, as opposed to the weapons just firing dead straight.

"I want to see if we get an improvement by reducing the range," said HB.

"I've had my down to seven fifty ever since we came back from France skipper." Mac spoke from the arm of a battered lounge chair. "It's worked well for me."

"Rubbish!" exclaimed Cavendish with a sneer. He was leaning against the opposite wall with his arms folded. "The official line is twelve hundred feet for a reason."

The atmosphere quickly became tense. Cavendish may have been addressing Mac, but his words were challenging his Commanding Officer.

"You've got to be dead astern or bloody lucky to hit anything if you're set to twelve hundred," Mac snapped defensively.

"If you are coming in on a beam attack against a Heinkel you need to be set at twelve hundred," countered Cavendish. The two men started to talk over each other and the volume of their voices increased as they pushed forward their arguments.

"Yes, but most of the time we're not dealing with bombers. It's bloody fighters. Seven fifty has got to be a better option," insisted Mac.

"Nonsense, we should be hitting the bombers and leaving the fighters alone!" replied Cavendish.

"And just how do you do that if there are swarms of 109s descending on you!"

The rest of us sat like Wimbledon spectators

watching an energetic rally on centre court.

"Gentlemen!" Hardy-Burton's voice stopped the argument abruptly. He looked hard at both pilots in turn.

"The official recommendation still stands at twelve hundred, however I've had this communication from Group." He prodded a piece of paper on the table. "Which states pilots are allowed to configure the harmonisation of the guns themselves. I will be setting mine to seven fifty." With that he pushed forward a packet of pamphlets. "I've also had this lot sent through." They were a set of Air Ministry publications for the estimation of range on fighters. There was an illustration of an aircraft flying through crosshairs and the words 'Bag the Hun!' in bright red letters across the top.

"I suggest we all refresh our memories." He cast a stern glance over us and left the room. Cavendish immediately disappeared through the other door. There was an exchange of astonished looks and a few whispers, then Mabel who had been lying by the stove suddenly rose to her feet, snorted and walked off in search of her master. Not wanting to be tied up in squadron politics I picked up one of the pamphlets and found an empty corner of the room.

I flicked through the publication. It was full of diagrams, tables and the odd amusing cartoon. It dawned on me that I'd been so preoccupied with fitting in with the other pilots I'd forgotten most of what I'd been taught about aerial warfare. I turned the pamphlet back to page one and decided to read it cover to cover. About two pages in I was interrupted by Mac.

"They're taking our aircraft over to the butts in half

an hour. It's best you come over and see how they're calibrated." He looked down at the pamphlet. To save some embarrassment I covered over the pencil notes I'd made in the margins.

"Swotting up?" I looked up at him and decided to throw myself at his mercy.

"Yes, but I've still not grasped how to set the sight properly?" It felt dangerous to admit my ignorance. Mac could laugh at me and question how I'd passed through operation training or worse still inform HB that one of the pilots was incapable of using his own gunsight. He did neither, instead he grabbed the pamphlet from my hands and sat down alongside me.

"You need to play the game on your terms." He flicked through the pages until he found a diagram of the gunsight. "A lot of pilots make the mistake of trying to adjust the sight in the middle of combat. What you need to do is set the sight to your preferred distance before the combat. Then wait for the enemy to come into your range. This way you can concentrate on flying and not fiddling with knobs and levers." For the next quarter of an hour he talked through the way he tackled the enemy in a dogfight. He was a good tutor and had a way of answering my questions without making me feel foolish.

When we left the Dispersal Hut the southern horizon had turned dark grey and an enormous cumulus cloud, heavy with rain, towered above the airfield. A strong wind had picked up and the change in pressure suggested a squall was heading our way.

The butts were a simple brick structure against which sand was banked. Here the tail planes of the Hurricanes were raised until the wings were level with the ground. Then the guns of aircraft would be adjusted and test fired.

Edwards and his crew had already raised Mac's aircraft into position. Mac jumped up on the wing where the armourer knelt beside the open gun bay.

"Have a look at this," he shouted back to me. I climbed up next to him and he talked me through the adjustments that were being made. When he was satisfied the angle was correct he jumped into the cockpit while the armourer and I slid down off the wing.

By now the wind was whipping round the butts and blowing a thin line of sand off the bank. Large spots of rain started to fall on the grey concrete. Mac gave a thumbs up from the cockpit and opened fire. The noise of the eight machine guns firing at once was immense. The loud burst was followed by the gentle ringing of the spent cartridge cases dropping to the ground. Mac made safe and jumped out to check the result. The armourer made another adjustment and the guns were tested again.

By now the squall was upon us. With the lashing rain, and the awesome sound of the Browning machine guns it felt as though we'd woken up Vulcan from a celestial slumber. We reconfigured and tested my aircraft afterwards. It was great fun pressing the button and watching the sand flying upwards as the rounds buried themselves deep in the butts. When we were happy that the aircraft were prepared we walked back to the Dispersal Hut to dry out. The storm had abated and a freshness was emanating from the earth.

Chapter 8
The Pictures

Freddie suggested we visit the cinema in Epping. Permission was granted and transport was laid on with one of the familiar Bedford lorries picking us from the mess. Our first stop was the local police station where we reported to an aging constable and told him our plans for the evening. This arrangement meant that if we were needed back at the squadron anyone could reach us via the local constabulary. It was Freddie who remarked on how strange it was to start an evening in the police station as opposed to ending it there.

The Empire Cinema with its white painted stonework and decorative pillars stood like a roman temple in the middle of Epping High Street. A line of people, fenced in by a velvet rope, queued from the top of the limestone steps like pilgrims waiting to worship at the site of a holy relic. As the queue shuffled through into the foyer, Freddie, who was out in front, gave a low pitched whistle through his teeth. He was staring at the usherette who stood selling cigarettes next to the kiosk.

"Vector One Eighty boys. Tally Ho…" he whispered.

The girl was certainly very striking. She wore a black uniform with gold piping that lined the lapels. Her bust was pushed up and out by a heavily reinforced brassiere which overhung the tray of tobacco like a granite outcrop. Her hair was bleached blonde and her lips were defined by bright red lipstick. She wasn't elegant, but her appearance had a tantalising air of promiscuity about her, which undoubtedly earned her a fair amount of male attention.

"Hello there." Freddie lowered his voice by a full octave. "I'll have a pack of Craven A."

"That'll be three and six," she said as she searched for the packet on the tray.

"I suppose you get to watch all the new films, that must be a real perk." Freddie attempted to engage in harmless small talk.

"Yeah, but then after a while they get boring." She handed him the packet.

"Do you work late?"

"Nah not really, I finish at eight." She flapped her long eye lashes at him. "But I must be home by ten."

'The Home Guard claim their first victim by shooting down a Dornier with rifle fire.' The enthusiastic voice of the Newsreel announcer resounded around the theatre as footage of soldiers examining the wreckage of an aircraft projected onto the screen.

'Now a well earned tribute to the men of the anti aircraft defences.' The pictures went on to show a battery of artillery guns firing into the air.

"Ten to one they were firing at us." Lanky whispered in the darkness and there were a few muffled laughs. I lit one of the cigarettes that Freddie had bought and watched the smoke swirl gently upwards into the beam of the projector. The newsreels ended and the main feature started.

The film was 'Rebecca', a psychological thriller based in a strangely gothic looking Cornwall. I was intrigued by the plot and found myself engrossed with the performance when Freddie suddenly got up and squeezed past me. I looked up at him curiously.

"Got to go," he whispered "It's just gone eight and she's got to be home by ten." He winked an eye and disappeared into the darkness. Lanky shook his head in disbelief.

Back on screen Joan Fontaine was succumbing to Laurence Olivier's charms. I watched her through the haze of tobacco smoke. She had such an elegance about her and a sexuality that was far more subtle than the usherette.

When the film ended we found Freddie leaning against the columns outside. On his cheek he wore a smear of red lipstick like a badge of honour. In the back of the Bedford he gave a widely exaggerated report on his foray into female territory.

"Do you reckon you'll see her again?" I asked.

"Doubt it, she's supposed to be engaged to a sailor," Freddie replied.

"You don't stand a chance," Lanky interrupted. "The Navy has got far better uniforms."

We arrived back at the station with just enough time for a beer in the mess. Boisterously we piled out of the Bedford and straight into Warrant Officer Murray. Fumbling with our buttons we straighten ourselves out and stood to attention. Murray looked at us with disdainful eyes and twitching moustache. He walked over to Freddie and studied the red mark on his cheek.

"Wearing make up? I didn't have you down as one of those types." Freddie blushed with embarrassment. "Get it cleaned off immediately!" Murray snapped and then strutted off.

Before going to sleep that night I wrote home. It was a difficult letter to pen as I had to avoid any security details and I didn't want my family to think I was in any danger. This left me little to write about except the Essex countryside and the unpredictable weather. When I finished, I took a sip of brandy and reflected on what had happened over the last week. I had never experienced such a range of emotions and feelings in such a short space of time. Just a few days ago I'd felt overawed by the duties I was expected to carry out. Now the early mornings and regular patrols were becoming second nature. Visits to the pub, unscheduled cricket matches and our trip to the pictures had helped me adjust to squadron life.

As I dragged my fountain pen across the writing paper I had no idea how fortunate I'd been to arrive at North Weald when I did. The Luftwaffe had been restraining its actions against mainland Britain while they prepared for a major offensive. This lull in the battle had given me time to find my feet and settle in. While I wrote about how bad the train journey was to Epping and how good the food was in the mess, Herman Göring, the Commander in Chief of the Luftwaffe, sat impatiently in Berlin waiting for four days of good weather in which he could destroy the Royal Air Force.

Chapter 9
First Blood

It was difficult to estimate how many colours were in that early morning sky. The horizon was blood red, the silhouetted clouds were almost black and high above the atmosphere was a deep blue. I sat in the cockpit of my Hurricane marvelling at the palette of colours while we waited for the last few aircraft to start up. Presently we were airborne and flying into that ethereal horizon.

Almost as our wheels had parted from the ground we had been directed on a vector that took us south west. We crossed directly over London and I allowed myself a few seconds of sightseeing. Boats and barges littered the river beneath an army of lattice work cranes. The river glistened in the morning sun as it snaked its way from the west. Even from this height the city looked grey and dirty. I spotted Waterloo station being fed by a network of railway lines. Rising in its gothic form was the Houses of Parliament with Saint Stephen's tower and Big Ben casting an impressive shadow towards Whitehall. Somewhere there, nestled behind the Portland stone facades would be Churchill, probably having breakfast. What decision would he be making down there today that would affect all of us tomorrow? The cream chimneys of Battersea power station smoked away next to Grosvenor Railway Bridge, over which a freight train was heading north.

We carried on and the city started to ebb away. Above the South Downs we climbed to fifteen thousand feet. It had started to become misty, but I could make out the English channel no more than twenty miles away. When you're on the ground it's easy to forget that Britain is an Island, but in an aircraft you don't have to fly for very long before you find the sea.

These patrols were becoming very routine and slightly monotonous. My concentration started to wane and I found myself slipping into random thoughts about nothing in particular. I was quickly woken from this reverie by a voice on the radio.

"Dead ahead skipper, convoy about four miles out in the oggin" said Doc.

In the far distance I could see the faint outline of four merchant ships that were chugging along the channel past Selsey Bill. Above them and at a similar height to us was a swarm of little black dots.

"Bandits! Eleven o'clock high," came another voice. One at a time the dots started to dive down towards the ships below. They were obviously Stuka dive bombers. We powered on as quickly as we could, but the attack was well under way before we arrived. Remembering Mac's instructions I clicked the range dial into position and set the gun sight.

A great white flash emanated from one of the ships as the Stukas claimed a direct hit. This was immediately followed by a great column of smoke which rose into the band of mist. Even from this distance we could see the confusion and panic that was going on down below. The convoy was being escorted by two naval destroyers. Both of which were firing their anti-aircraft guns and filling the sky with small black clouds of shrapnel.

One of the destroyers had turned hard to starboard leaving behind a great curving wake of foam. A Stuka attacked, dropping a bomb alongside the destroyer with a huge splash of water. Another came in low towards the ship strafing the deck with machine gun fire.

We were in good range when HB called "Tally Ho."

I stayed in formation with Mac as we dived down into the battle. Another Stuka was just starting its bombing run. We came around in a long turn that brought the sun behind us. The Stuka let go of his deadly cargo and pulled up from the dive. He was now perfectly in range of our guns. I saw a piece of metal splinter off the Stuka's tailplane as Mac opened fire. Then unexpectedly, Mac broke up and right. I was confused by his movement, but it left me with a perfect shot. The slow vulture-like dive bomber filled the orange ring in my gunsight. I was that close I could clearly see the rear gunner. He was bobbing up and down in the cockpit while the barrel of the machine gun waved about in the air. He was changing the magazine. I seized the opportunity and pressed the gun button. I felt the familiar judder of the guns. The canopy of the dive bomber shattered and a line of small yellow flashes ran along the fuselage. My bullets tore off a large metal panel which flew upwards into the air stream and passed me. Puffs of smoke burst from under the engine cowling. The Stuka pitched forward and dived, the pilot was either dead or seriously injured. I'd overshot and had to turn hard to catch sight of it again. It was leaving behind a trail of smoke and steam as it plummeted down.

Then the aircraft corrected itself and it looked like it was about to make a perfect landing on the sea, but the undercarriage caught the waves and it cartwheeled on to its back. I banked my wing to watch the sky-blue underbelly of the forlorn bomber being sucked into the water.

I was amazed at how quick and easy it had been to blast the Stuka out of the sky. I circled around the spot where it had sunk, wondering if by some miracle the crew would surface, but there was no sign of life.

The Stukas had done their job well. The bridge of the cargo ship was obscured by billowing smoke and large orange flames that licked out around the deck. The destroyer was now trying to manoeuvre alongside. Someone was dowsing the metal work with a pathetically small fire hose. Other men were running back and forth. I winced as one jumped from the rails of the cargo ship into the water between the two ships. The scene looked terrifying, I was grateful to be in the air and not down there.

Over my port wing I caught sight of a Messerschmitt 109 diving towards the west. He was far enough away for me not to worry about, but if there was one there were probably others around. I looked over my shoulder and sure enough about seven hundred feet off of my port beam was a 109 heading straight for me. I instantly snapped into a half roll and turned.

What a fool! I'd been completely distracted by the spectacle of the flaming cargo ship that I'd forgotten I was in the middle of a dogfight. I'd been flying straight and level leaving myself wide open to attack. I pulled hard into the turn hoping the 109 would overshoot, but he didn't. There in my mirror I could see his brilliant yellow nose and white spinner. My options were limited. We were barely a thousand feet high. If I climbed I would lose speed and present myself as a juicy target for him. I could dive, but he would be faster than me and there was little chance I could outrun him. My only option was to turn and turn tighter than he could. I pulled back on the stick further and further. The world went by in a blur of green, grey and blue. It was impossible to make out what was sea and what was sky. Harder and harder I pulled, expecting that any moment his bullets would punch through my cockpit. I turned so tightly the g force pushed me hard into the seat and my limbs became heavy. I was amazed my aircraft didn't tear apart. The weight of my head pushed against my neck and the world started to fade as my brain became starved of that crucial oxygen. It felt as though I'd rotated a hundred times, but it was probably no more than three hard turns. As I started to black out I believe my grip on the control column loosened as I was suddenly aware of the aircraft's attitude changing and the g force subsiding. The Messerschmitt had gone from my mirror. I checked left and right, but couldn't see him. The cargo ship was still belching out black smoke, but the sky was clear of aircraft. Where had they gone? I didn't want to hang around, so I pushed the throttle forward and dived for the coastline.

Like a startled rabbit I darted from side to side terrified that at any moment the Messerschmitt would reappear in my mirror. It was a relief to get back over land where I felt I might be less conspicuous.

It dawned on me that I didn't know exactly where I was. There were no other aircraft to follow and stupidly I'd not brought a map with me. What was it HB said? "Never go anywhere without a map."

I had become so used to flying over the Thames Estuary, where I now knew all the landmarks, that I'd not needed to use a map for days. Fortunately the sky was clear enough for me to try and navigate by sight. I assumed that if I flew northeast eventually I'd come to London, from there on finding North Weald would be easy.

I did have two concerns though. The first was flying straight into an anti-aircraft barrage and being shot at by our own over-enthusiastic gunners. The second was the embarrassment of having to land at another airfield and ask for directions home. This kind of faux pas would be a real black mark against me. My best defence against being shot at was to fly low where it would be easier to identify me as friendly.

I raced back over the South Downs at five hundred feet. The rolling landscape with its fields of crops and dark green beech trees passed beneath me. Eventually I came across a trainline. I figured that the line would run into London so I gained at little altitude and followed it until the shimmering grey capital came into sight.

I flew over what I believe was Richmond Park. Just north of there I found the Thames at Putney. By now the fear of pursuit had disappeared so I climbed up and followed the river towards the City, then I turned north into familiar territory. I took a wide circuit around the airfield as two other Hurricanes were landing at the same time. I lowered the flaps and let the aircraft bump gently onto the grass. I taxied up to the Dispersal Hut and shut the engine down.

I sat still, staring up at the sky for a good minute. I was breathing heavily and from under my helmet beads of sweat were running down my face. My trousers were damp and I thought for one embarrassing moment that I'd wet myself, but it was all just perspiration. One of the riggers appeared on the wing. He had a friendly face with a set of mismatched teeth and ears that seemed they were a size too large for his face.

"You alright there Sarge?" he asked.

"Yes, just give me a minute."

"Any damage to report?"

I thought back to the stress and strain I'd just put the aircraft through and then affectionately touched the control column. It was then I realised how strong the bond between pilot and aircraft could become. Like the relationship a Cavalry Officer has with his horse.

"No, she handled beautifully," I replied with a smile.

I undid my straps, heaved myself out of the cockpit and climbed down slowly. At the Dispersal I stood and watched as more of the squadron arrived and taxied in. Mabel ran back and forth excitedly as though she was checking each one of us in.

Freddie offered me a cigarette without saying a word. I smiled and took one. It felt as though I'd worked a full day and yet my wristwatch said it was only seven am.

Mac had arrived and was walking towards us with his Mae West slung over his shoulder. He pushed his dishevelled hair away from his eyes and grinned.

"I thought you were a goner. That 109 was on you like a bad rash." He produced his own packet of cigarettes and lit one.

"I just turned and hoped for the best. I didn't see what happened to him." I did not want to highlight the fact I'd left myself wide open for attack.

"I think Doc had a squirt at him and he scuttled off." Mac took a lung full of smoke and exhaled upwards.

Right on cue the familiar Humber Staff car arrived and Shelton climbed out with his clipboard ready in hand.

"Busy morning for you chaps." He took a pencil from his inside pocket.

"You creeps know what we've been up to before we've bloody well done it," complained Warwick who had also just arrived. "Put me down for half a Stuka. Delaney started on him but I finished him off."

"Anyone else have any luck?" asked Freddie.

"Sommers lost his cherry I believe," quipped Mac. I was so concerned with escaping the Messerschmitt I'd completely forgotten about the Stuka I'd hit.

"Well only half of one," I looked at Mac.

"Nonsense, I couldn't get a bead on him so I pulled out."

I know that I saw Mac hit that aircraft. He had every right to claim half a kill, but he didn't. Then it all became clear, he'd broken off on purpose to give me a chance. But then that was Mac's style, he took more pride in his subordinates' success than his own. No other pilot would ever have a greater impression on me than him.

"What happened to Lanky?" asked Freddie. I looked at him with a puzzled expression.

"Was he hit?"

"I didn't see him." Mac shrugged his shoulders. An airman appeared and offered us hot coffee from a battered tea tray.

"I saw Long get it pretty badly." Warwick sipped his coffee and then wiped his moustache with the sleeve of his flying suit. "He got out, I saw a chute open."

Much later I found out what had happened to Lanky. He was flying in Green Section and when the order for attack was given he ploughed straight into the diving Stukas. We were all so focused on the convoy and the Stukas that no one saw the 109's who were flying top cover. As we descended on the Stukas, they descended on us. A single 109 tore through the section hitting both Warwick and Lanky with cannon shells. Warwick only took one hit which sailed through the fuselage missing all vital components. Lanky was less fortunate. Seven or eight shells hit his fuselage. Two hit the engine, stopping it dead, another went through the cockpit taking a large slice of flesh from his thigh with it.

His aircraft started to nose over, he managed to pull the stick back, but he was in agony. The cannon shells had also ruptured the forward fuel tank and petrol was dribbling onto his legs. With no engine, hardly any control over the aircraft and the likelihood of a fire in the cockpit he decided it was time to go. He mustered enough strength to force the canopy open and pull the pin from the seat harness. However, when he went to launch himself out he found he was almost completely paralysed from the waist down.

He tried again to pull himself up with his hands, but it was no good. He was rapidly losing altitude and had to do something. He pulled on the control column and took the aircraft into a slow roll. When he was completely inverted he gripped the cockpit sides again and fell out of the aircraft as he put it 'like a calf out of a pregnant heifer.' As he spun falling through the air he managed to grab the D ring and open the parachute. His Hurricane disappeared into the water and he floated down close to the destroyer. Wrapped up in the parachute straps and with half his thigh missing he struggled in the water and was going under for a third time when he was rescued by a launch that had been deployed by the destroyer.

He was saved from drowning, but it would be a full year before he could walk again.

Shelton was very interested in my Stuka kill and interrogated me for a good ten minutes. I found it taxing to recall all the details of what had happened in that frantic few minutes of combat. When he had finished with me I sidled off to the crew room where I found a comfortable chair. I kicked my legs over the arm and made myself comfortable. Despite some resistance I let myself fall into a deep sleep.

The shrill bell of the telephone woke me with a start. I was on my feet before the corporal had time to pick up the receiver. I could tell from the strained expression on his face we were about to be scrambled. I grabbed my helmet and was running for my aircraft as he shouted to the rest of the pilots. I strapped on my parachute and climbed into the cockpit.

We rolled down the runway and lifted once more into the Essex sky. I had no idea of how long I'd been asleep, it could have been five minutes, it could have been five hours. I checked my wristwatch. It was only half past eight, by God they were keeping us busy today.

We were vectored towards the east this time and over the familiar landscape of the Thames Estuary. Sector control instructed us to form up with another squadron of Hurricanes and wait for a formation of enemy bombers heading our way. We found the other squadron and after some confused messages took position above them. Both squadrons flew round and round for a good half hour, the enemy never showed up. We returned to North Weald frustrated by the pointless operation.

On the ground I found myself getting a little jittery. I noticed that some of the other pilots were getting restless too, I think we all felt something ominous was brewing. I kept looking towards the crew room telephone convinced that it was about to start ringing. I was glad to see Mac and Warwick start another game of 'tea chest' cricket, just the distraction I needed.

At midday we flew a patrol over Kent. We saw a flight of Spitfires intercept a small group of Junkers in the distance, but apart from that the patrol was unremarkable.

It was customary for us to split into our respective sections when landing. Mac was leading Yellow Section on the final approach when out of nowhere another Hurricane cut straight across his nose forcing him to pull up to avoid a collision.

The pilot of the offending Hurricane was Cavendish, he was totally out of position. Mac brought the section around the circuit once more giving Cavendish space to land safely. By the time we landed he was standing by his aircraft.

"What the bloody hell did you think you were doing?" He shouted at Mac as soon as the din of engines had died.

"What was I doing? You were the one out of position!" Mac retorted. Cavendish snarled like a rabid dog and walked off.

Outside the crew room Warwick tapped his pipe out on the windowsill.

"Well I need a bloody drink tonight."

"I second that," said Freddie. "We've got to

celebrate Sommers breaking his duck."

"An evening at the George then." Mac pointed at me "And drinks are on you."

Chapter 10
Fanshaw

The George and Dragon Public House was far better suited to a large group of rowdy pilots than the local country inns. It stood halfway down Epping High Street, not far from the Empire Cinema.

That distinct smell of woodchip wallpaper impregnated with tobacco and stale beer emanated from the open door. Inside, the saloon was already busy with evening drinkers. Little groups of men were dotted around discussing current affairs and moaning about the price of beer. A few couples occupied the quiet corners. The husbands looked vacant while the women gossiped about their social lives. A trio of engineers in khaki shifted away from the bar when they saw us approaching.

The barmaid was an attractive middle aged woman with an ample bosom, pink lipstick and hair swept up in a pompadour style. She watched us from behind the bar with her hands on her hips and a fiery look in her eye.

"You boys going to behave tonight?" It was more of a statement than a question.

"Absolutely my dearest." Warwick smiled at her. "We're always on best behaviour."

"Well you weren't last time you were here." Evidently the squadron had visited the George several times before. With a brisk flick of her dishcloth she took our order and a round of drinks was passed down the bar.

"I propose a toast," announced Aussie who'd picked up the first pint of ale. "I reckon we claimed

our 15th kill today. So here's to the 15th Nazi and…"
He turned to me. "Sommers' first blood." There was a
hearty cheer and a momentary silence as we swigged
our drinks.

The beer quenched my thirst and refreshed me more
than I expected. I felt the muscles in my body soften as
the alcohol seeped into my bloodstream. The first
round of drinks disappeared and was quickly replaced
by another.

The saloon, now packed with bodies, was becoming
hot and humid. I loosened my tie.

"Improperly dressed again!" said a voice from
behind me. I turned to see HB and the Adjutant
standing at the bar. I quickly grappled with my top
button and tried to readjust my tie.

HB laughed. "Alright Sommers, stand down."

"Can we get you a drink sir?" asked Mac who had
also spotted HB. "It's Aussie's round." he added.

"Thank you. A scotch and soda, please."

As the barmaid rummaged through the bottles on
the shelf, HB addressed the small knot of people who
had now formed around him.

"Well done chaps, another good day." He lowered
his voice. "Just take it easy tonight, we've got another
early start tomorrow." From behind the bar his scotch
arrived. He took the glass and held it aloft.
"Gentlemen, 506." We all raised our glasses and
repeated the toast.

There was a crash of piano keys and I turned to see
Warwick sitting at an old walnut upright. His pipe, as
always, was clenched between his teeth and his pint
glass had been precariously placed on top of the piano.
He started to play a classical piece that I recognised,
but couldn't name.

HB and the Adjutant stayed for one drink, engaged in a bit of banter and then slipped off without ceremony.

Mac and I were discussing what had happened that morning when a man pushed between us.

"Now there's someone who'll have a spare smoke." The man smacked his hand on Mac's shoulder.

"You can bugger off. You still owe me a quid from last month," replied Mac. The man smiled and Mac reluctantly offered up a packet.

"Be careful what you say around this man, Sommers," warned Mac. "This is James Fanshaw, failed author, divorcee and gossip columnist. Anything you say tonight may end up in print tomorrow."

Fanshaw looked at me.

"Actually my job title is West End Correspondent, but Mac's right on the other two points."

He had a striking presence. His dark hair, dark eyes and rugged features hinted at a Celtic bloodline. His pinstripe suit was well tailored and well worn. He was suave in his manner, but there was an air of long hours and missed deadlines about him.

"You're quite far from the West End." I pointed out.

"Yes divorce will do that to you," he laughed. 'I like to get out of the city and enjoy the country air."

"Ha! Poppycock!" said Mac. "His wife left for America with his best man and most of his money. He now has to lodge with his Aunt." Fanshaw grinned back at Mac.

"Well, yes I suppose that's true."

"Which newspaper do you write for?" I asked.

"The Sketch at the moment, but hopefully not for long."

"What's it like up in town these days?" Mac asked.

"The place is full of sandbags and gasmasks. It's pitch black in the evening and every square inch is covered with posters about the war. But it's as busy as ever and nobody seems to be worried about anything." Fanshaw lit the cigarette Mac had given him. He looked at me deeply.

"So how's the war going for you boys?" The question caught me off guard, we'd been constantly warned about giving away information to civilians. To my relief Mac butted in and answered for me.

"Well we joined the Royal Air Force to fly and that's what we're doing," he said abruptly. Fanshaw laughed again.

"You know after this is all over you should go into politics."

"Never." Mac shook his head. Aussie barged into the centre of the group.

"Sounds like it's getting depressing here. Mac, it's your round."

Just then the frosted glass door opened and in walked Freddie with his arms around two girls. One of them was the peroxide blond usherette from the Empire, the other was a brunette who wore a dark grey beret.

"Blimey Fuller, you work quickly, I didn't see you leave," Aussie called out.

"Everybody - I'd like you to meet Ada and Joan," announced Freddie, as if he was introducing a cabaret act. There were various wolf whistles and inappropriate noises from the bar. The tempo of the piano changed and Warwick started playing some old music hall numbers. Freddie walked over to where we were standing.

"You remember Ada from last night don't you." He winked at me.

"Yes, how do you do?" I introduced myself rather too formally. The two girls smiled back.

"Look after them for a moment, will you? I want to get us some drinks," said Freddie and he pushed his way through the crowd. I was left staring at the girls and after a slightly awkward silence I spoke.

"Do you both live in Epping?" I asked. Ada looked at me with her wide eyes.

"Yeah, about five minutes walk from here."

I nodded with interest and sipped my drink while I tried to come up with a better line of conversation. Joan looked around the room, then to the brevet on my chest.

"You all pilots?" She asked.

"Yes we are." I tried to sound casual.

"Didn't you have another mate with you last night?" Ada asked. I'd forgotten about Lanky, it was only that morning he'd been shot down and yet it seemed like he left the squadron years ago.

"Oh Lanky, he can't make it out tonight." I skirted around the subject, I didn't want to talk about what had happened to him. There was a shout from the other side of the room, it was Fanshaw approaching the piano.

"Stop murdering the ivories and give me a go." He took off his suit jacket revealing a set of bright red braces. With a friendly shove he pushed Warwick off the stall and sat himself down. He stretched his fingers and started to play Love for Sale. I'd only really heard jazz standards played on the radio before. I was instantly captivated by the music and his playing. His left hand plodded back and forth while his right lazily wandered around creating a melody. Every now and then he would reach to the far end and stab a high note. It seemed effortless and yet complex at the same time. I found my toes starting to tap.

"You like jazz?" I hadn't realised Joan was watching me. I looked at her, she had incredible green eyes that sparkled above her freckled cheeks.

"Yes, do you?"

"I love it," she said, "my sister is a nurse on the Queen Mary, she's always bringing back records from New York."

We spoke for a time about the different musicians we'd heard while Fanshaw played on. It was novel for me to find a common interest with a girl that wasn't the weather.

The rest of the evening passed by in snatches of conversation and one line jokes. Before long the barmaid called time and we all poured out on the street in a large crowd.

Joan looked at me. "Maybe we can meet at the pictures sometime?" I was taken aback by her forwardness. I'd assumed it was my job to make the first move.

"Yes, I think I'd like that." I answered. I looked over and saw Freddie and Ada had tucked themselves into a shop doorway. I think they were trying for an impassioned embrace, but in the moonlight it looked more like they were wrestling.

A man on a bicycle appeared at the top of the high street. He was silhouetted against the reflected moonlight and I thought at first he was wearing a trench coat but as he got closer I saw it was a dressing gown. On his feet he wore a pair of slippers. He peddled slowly and looked as though he was searching for something.

"Oh my God!" exclaimed Joan. "That's Ada's Dad, we were supposed to be home by ten. He must have come out looking for us." With that she turned and ran towards the young lovers, grabbed Ada's arm and the two girls disappeared into the darkness. The cyclist stopped when he reached us and peered into the crowd. Freddie emerged from the shop doorway with his tunic undone. He adjusted his trousers, looked up at the man and smiled.

"Evening. Nice night for a ride." he remarked. A few laughs and chortles emanated from the crowd. The man grunted and cycled on. As he disappeared down the road I whispered to Freddie.

"I thought Ada had a boyfriend in the Navy?"

"Yeah." Freddie straightened his tie. "But he's not home for another six weeks."

I drank too much that evening, but with every round of alcohol, the anxious feeling that had been swelling up inside seemed to fade. When I stumbled into my room I found that all Lanky's kit had been removed.

The small room suddenly felt very large and sparse.

Chapter 11
Tangmere

The first phase of the Battle had come to an end. Until now the Luftwaffe had concentrated on attacking shipping convoys that were vital to Britain's survival. Goering had hoped to choke the island by blockading the seas that surrounded it. However, if a German invasion was still to be successful the Royal Air Force still had to be neutralised.

Now the Luftwaffe prepared for Alderangriff or 'Operation Eagle Attack' in which British airfields, radar stations and aircraft factories would become the primary targets.

I'm pretty certain I was still drunk when the duty corporal woke me a few hours later. Hot toast and a cigarette did something to soak up the alcohol, but the world was still slightly out of focus when I climbed into the Bedford. Freddie didn't look much better.

"Best thing you can do is take a lung-full of oxygen when you get in the cockpit." he said as I looked at him through heavy eyelids. I took his advice and the first thing I did after stumbling into my aircraft was to put on my mask, turn on the taps and take a lung full of gas. It certainly woke me up although I was starting to feel queasy.

We saw no sign of the enemy that day and apart from chasing off a few reconnaissance patrols the following days were also quiet.

It was a Friday morning when we arrived as usual for the first light patrol. Edwards was waiting for me by the Dispersal Hut.

"I'm afraid your machine is still in the shed." he said. Every evening the aircraft were taken by the erks and checked over. My Hurricane had been due its twenty hour maintenance which involved changing engine oil and a thorough check of the flying controls.

"They found bits of metal in the sump," Edwards continued. "We couldn't take any chances so the lads are doing an engine change as we speak." It was frustrating, but changing an engine was a difficult job and I know the fitters would have been working through the night to get it finished.

With no aircraft to fly I watched the squadron take off and head into the grey rain clouds. I found a comfortable spot in the crew room and decided to sleep off the rest of my hangover.

I woke to find the Adjutant standing over me.

"Your kite is going to be out of action for another hour or two." I sat up rubbing my blood shot eyes. "In the meantime there's a Hurricane that's been assigned to us down at Tangmere. I want you to pop down and bring it back here."

"Yes Sir." I stood up and straightened my tunic. "How do I get to Tangmere?"

"There's an Anson due in twenty minutes. He's taking one of the intelligence officers down to Kent. I called the Ops Room and they told him to drop you of enroute."

Fifteen minutes later I found myself waiting with Shelton, the intelligence officer, at the other end of the airfield.

The little Avro Anson in its brown and green camouflage buzzed over the hangars and landed softly on the runway. It taxied up to us and turned into wind. The pilot throttled back and brought the two Cheetah engines to idle. The Anson was a sweet looking aircraft that had a variety of uses. It had a wide fuselage and low pointed nose which made it look like a large penny loafer. It had originally been developed for maritime reconnaissance, but it was more common to see them being used to ferry personnel from place to place.

An odd shaped door, which was barely three feet high, opened above the trailing edge of the wing. It was difficult to squeeze in without putting your foot through the canvas. Inside, the fuselage allowed four passengers to sit down with plenty of room for their legs and baggage. Shelton with his briefcase and raincoat over his arm climbed in first. I clambered up to the front and spoke to the pilot. He was a middle-aged man wearing the rank of flying officer.

"Just the two of you?" He shouted over the sound of the idling engines.

"Yes Sir," I confirmed.

"Good stuff. I'll drop you at Tangmere first. I shan't shut down. Just jump out when we've stopped."

Shelton looked nervous. He clutched his briefcase like a commuter in a packed train carriage. I sat down opposite. Through the open cockpit I watched as we moved across the airfield.

It was the first time I'd been flown by another pilot since my basic training and I couldn't help feeling nervous at not being in control. I found myself studying his movements and had to force myself to look away. I was amazed at how much slower the aircraft felt compared to the Hurricane as we ran down the runway and lifted off. There was a whine and clunk as the undercarriage retracted.

Tangmere was a station situated on the coast of

Sussex, not far from Chichester. Two squadrons of fighters were based there and like us they'd been fighting hard over the channel for the past month.

To get to Tangmere with the least resistance, the pilot of the Anson flew a dog leg course. First we headed west for several miles and then south. This avoided the anti-aircraft defences that were placed all around London. I noticed Shelton had his eyes closed and I thought for a moment that he was sleeping, but he opened them and he saw me looking at him.

"Can't stand the take offs and landings," he explained. "I'm all right in the air, but it's the bit either end I hate."

We flew at a low altitude, partly to prevent being shot at and partly to avoid the low cloud base which was quickly dispersing. The Anson had been designed as an observation machine and had two sets of windows which ran down the fuselage and afforded a terrific view for any passengers. Shelton, still clutching his briefcase, nodded towards the ground.

"Uxbridge," he said. "They'll be busy down there today."

Uxbridge was the operations centre for Eleven Group which defended the South East of England. Information on enemy raiders from radar stations and observation posts was filtered into a top secret bunker here and then orders were issued to different fighter squadrons within the group. We were one of those squadrons.

"Do you think the Jerries will try and invade us?" I asked. It was a question that had been debated by many people over the past few weeks, but I thought that if anyone understood the real state of play it was likely to be an intelligence officer.

"It's hard to tell." He mused. "They've got to get across the channel first. Even if they can knock us out of the air, moving thousands of troops in slow moving barges across thirty miles of water would be very difficult. The navy would decimate them. Then if they could land, they'd have to get a foothold and then a supply route. It's a lot different from rolling over a border with tanks and dive bombers." He released his clutch on his briefcase and put it down between his knees.

"Are we're doing enough to keep them away?" I asked. He shrugged his shoulders.

"Maybe, but we can't really fathom what their strategy is. I think Hitler wants to put us in our place and then maybe seek a truce, but if we give in to him Lord knows what they'll do next. They could come down with the Italians into the Mediterranean. Some intelligence says Mussolini is eyeing up Greece already." He looked out of the window as the Thames Valley passed underneath. "We need to hit them hard and give them a bloody nose. Then maybe we can buy some time." he said thoughtfully.

We passed over Farnborough, Aldershot and onto the South Downs. After twenty five minutes or so the pilot shouted to me.

"We'll be there soon." I acknowledged him with a thumbs up.

Tangmere was nestled amongst a group of arable farms. The lush grass airfield stood out vividly against the brown and yellow harvested fields that surrounded it. As we came into land I noticed a group of Hurricanes being refuelled. Obviously a squadron had just returned from patrol. Our pilot taxied over towards the hangars, throttled back and turned to face me.

"Thanks," I shouted as I picked up my flying gear. Shelton looked up at me.

"Cheerio, good luck!" he gave me a smile. "No doubt I'll see you back at North Weald."

I opened the small door and climbed out. It slammed shut behind me and I checked the catch was secure. Through the fuselage windows I waved to the pilot. He throttled up immediately. The wash from the engines threw up a cloud of dust and dirt. I always seemed to arrive in a cloud of dust.

Almost all RAF stations were constructed from the same set of standard pattern buildings. Tangmere was no different. It consisted of several large Belfast hangars. These were wide buildings with brick walls and two large curved roofs that were formed from an intricate lattice of wood work. Behind these hangars were more buildings that serviced the airfield. It was like a small town and at any given time there could be around a thousand people living and working on a station like this.

I headed over to the first hangar on the western side. Just outside were the three Hurricanes I'd seen being refuelled. The aircraft had been brought into face each other and a bowser with its snake-like hoses parked in the centre. Two pilots stood with folded arms watching the aircraft being prepared.

I looked through the large open doors of the hangar, inside was a hive of activity. Four aircraft were sitting towards the front in different states of maintenance. On each one at least five men were working. A sergeant walked back and forth, drumming a cadence on his clipboard with a pencil. The floor was littered with metal panels and spare parts. Towards the back were other aircraft that appeared to have been discarded. A Tiger Moth with a mangled wing was collecting dust in the far corner, no doubt the result of an unsuccessful flying lesson. I spotted an officer who was inspecting the undercarriage of a Hurricane. I crouched down beside him.

"Excuse me sir." The officer shot me a glance and then looked back up into the wheel well.

"Yes?" he grunted.

"I've come to collect a Hurricane for 506 Squadron," I said. He muttered something about pipelines and then looked at me again.

"It won't be any of these." He nodded to the other Hurricanes. "You'll have to try one of the other hangars."

I retreated backwards from under the wing and on his advice tried the other hangars. In the last one I found a corporal carrying another clipboard.

"506 you say?" He ran his fingers down the list on his clipboard. "Oh yes, North Weald." He looked up and pointed to a Hurricane which stood on hydraulic jacks. "That's your bird, but she ain't ready." I looked at the aircraft.

"How long before she is?"

"Wilcox!" bellowed the corporal, "how long before you've got that prop finished?" There was a muffled shout from behind the engine cowling.

"Give us an hour, Corp."

"An hour?" I exclaimed.

"Well it's Hobson's choice mate," he said with a shrug. "The boys are working as fast as they can. But she'll need juice as well." His last few words were drowned out by the roar of engines as one of the squadrons took off down the runway. The corporal looked out of the open doors.

"Something going on today," he said "That lot has been up and down like a bloody yoyo." I had to agree with him that something felt odd about the atmosphere around the station, but I didn't know if Tangmere always felt like this. He looked back at me.

"Come back in an hour. We'll see what we can do." I relaxed my shoulders and with a sigh conceded to the suggestion.

I found the NAAFI wagon which was parked behind the hangars. I bought a large slice of bread pudding and a cup of strange looking tea. The hour passed agonisingly slowly, but I eventually saw the Hurricane was being pushed outside.

"She still needs fuel," said the Corporal "and the squadrons have got priority. As soon as they're done one of the bowsers will come over."

I put my flying gear into the cockpit and sat down on the arid grass. The weather had cleared and the warm sun beat down on my face.

In the sky above a buzzard with his large wings outstretched spiralled round and round on a thermal. A flock of seagulls had worked their way in land and were squawking to each other above the fields.

An engine fitter arrived with a step ladder and tin can. As he set about topping up the engine coolant he started to whistle a cheerful melody. As pleasant as it was to be sunning myself in Southern England I was eager to return to North Weald.

From the other end of the airfield a bell rang out and I heard someone shouting. One of the other squadrons was being scrambled. The pilots raced towards their aircraft, started their engines and then thundered down the runway. I watched as they headed towards Portsmouth.

Behind me I heard the door to one of the smaller buildings open. I turned to see two young women in uniform, carrying chairs and a folding table which they set around on a patch of grass. Another woman appeared with a black box, it was a gramophone. Two more arrived carrying sandwiches and flasks. They were obviously taking advantage of the good weather and lunching outside. One of the women opened the gramophone and removed a record from its brown paper sleeve. She flipped the black disc over in her hands and placed it on the turntable. She wound the handle several times and then lifted the needle onto the spinning record. There were a few crackles and the opening chords of a Charles Trenet song drifted out of the box.

Quand notre coeur fait Boum !
Tout avec lui dit Boum !

When our heart goes "Boom!"
Everything goes "Boom!" with it,

I watched the women for a while as they chatted and laughed. It seemed such a carefree and innocent scene.

The fuel bowser trundled over the grass and parked up by the Hurricane. The fitter had finished pouring the coolant from his can and was screwing up the cap.

The gramophone was suddenly drowned out by the unmistakable whine of an air raid siren which drifted up from the western end of the airfield. Almost immediately it was joined by another and the haunting wail echoed around the buildings. I shot to my feet.

"Don't worry about them," said the fitter who was

now climbing down his ladder. "They go off three times a day and nothing happens." He picked up his can and walked nonchalantly back towards the hangars. Nothing did happen, for a minute or two.

Across the fields the seagulls had risen higher, but higher still I saw a formation of aircraft. They were too far away for my naked eye to identify them, but something about their movements made me feel uneasy. The lead aircraft must have been at least twelve thousand feet high and heading directly towards the airfield. I watched as it passed over and then suddenly rolled inverted. I'd seen this manoeuvre before, this was a Stuka starting its bombing run. Sure enough its nose pitched down and it started diving towards us.

There was a crackle, it was the station Tannoy. From a set of speakers fixed to the building behind me came an urgent voice.

"Take cover! Take cover! Take cover!"

Air raid precautions had been a widely discussed subject since the start of the war. As a lot of the official advice seemed to contradict itself, I'd formulated my own ideas on what to do if I was caught in the middle of an air raid. I decided on two rules. The first was to get away from any large building, the second was to keep clear of any object that might prove a tempting target for the enemy. At present I was standing between a very large aircraft hangar and a bowser full of fuel which had just arrived. I suddenly felt very vulnerable and impulsively sprinted towards a small mound of earth a hundred yards away. Halfway across I heard the repetitive bangs of a Bofors anti-aircraft opening up. I flung myself headlong over the mound and laid flat. I twisted my head just in time to see a five hundred pound bomb separate from the Stuka. Even at that distance I could make out the bulbous black shape with its metal fins. The Stuka pulled up out of its dive, but my eyes followed the bomb as it fell dead straight towards the ground. It landed behind the hangars. A second later there was an almighty crack and then a resonating deep boom. The earth shook and the ground rippled. A furious cloud of smoke and dust funnelled up high from where the bomb had detonated. Fragments of debris which had been raised high by the explosion rained down. The sound of breaking glass came from all directions.

I looked towards where the women had been sitting. Two of the chairs had been turned over, the table was on its side and the gramophone had broken in two. From what I could make out it looked like the women had taken refuge in a slit trench not far from the building.

Another Stuka let go of its bomb and there was a second explosion, this time towards the other end of the airfield. I saw the first attacker had pulled around and was now heading back towards the hangars. The Stuka was equipped with a single deadly bomb. Once that had been dropped some pilots would run in at a lower level and open fire with their machine guns. I realised that if this pilot was coming in to attack again there was every chance I'd be caught in his aim. I leapt up and ran for the slit trench. It was deeper than I'd expected and I ended up somersaulting over a wall of sandbags and landing on my back. As I tried to scramble to my feet another bomb exploded close to the first. This dislodged a fair amount of earth from the sides of the trench and knocked me back to the ground. For one dreadful second I thought I might be buried alive. I scrambled up again. The trench was about twenty feet long at the other end huddled together were the five women.

To my left the Stuka passed by with its guns blazing. Hundreds of small puffs of dust erupted as the bullets raked the airfield. I'd been wise to move.

Above yet another Stuka dived down to attack. His bomb landed further away but the explosion was far fiercer. I could see a group of men struggling to close the large doors on the second hangar. I couldn't understand why, but I assumed they were trying to protect the aircraft inside. As I peered over the sandbags another bomb fell. This one penetrated the roof of the hangar. There was a ground shaking boom and I instinctively ducked down. When I looked up a second later, the men, the large door and half of the building had disappeared. A man in blue overalls jumped into the trench behind me. We looked at each other, but said nothing.

The Bofors guns that had been firing at the Stukas were now joined by machine gun fire as other crews took up their battle positions. With no weapon and no means of defence except hiding I felt impotent and frustrated. I stuck my head over the sandbags and looked towards the Hurricane that I'd been sent to collect. Could I get it airborne? It was tempting. I'd have to run to it, climb in and start the engine on my own. That could take several minutes, in which time I'd be a sitting duck. Even if I was successful in getting airborne I had no idea how much fuel or ammunition she had on board. Reluctantly I decided to stay in the trench.

Another bomb sent sheets of corrugated iron barrelling through the air. The ground shook again, sending more dust into the atmosphere. Flames rose high from one of the hangars. One of the young women started to cry out.

"Oh God! Oh God! Oh God!" She sat at the bottom of the trench with her knees brought up and her hands covering her ears. Keeping as low as possible, I crawled along towards her and tried to speak over the din of gunfire.

"It's OK, it's going to be all right." My words did little to comfort her. An aircraft flew directly over our heads. It was so low that it kicked up loose sand from the top of the trench. The noise of the engines and the sinister shadow that it cast over us was terrifying. It moved so quickly that I didn't see whether it was British or German. I cowered against the side of the trench in case a volley of machine gun fire was going to follow. The woman screamed out again. This time her shout was incoherent. Another woman, a corporal, tried to comfort her, but she recoiled at her touch and fell against my leg. Never had I seen such terror in a person's face. Her complexion was grey and her lips contorted. Her large brown eyes appeared transfixed on something that wasn't there. As she looked up her wailing softened to a whimper.

"For God's sake pull yourself together!" snapped the female corporal. She looked up at me and pointed towards some trees.

"There's a shelter over there," she said. "It's bigger and further from the buildings. I think we should get her in there." I looked up towards the sky. The first wave of Stukas had dispersed, but over towards the south another formation was approaching.

"We'd better go now." I suggested. The corporal stood up and shouted to the other women.

"Make for the shelter over there. Go now!" They scrambled to their feet and out of the trench. The corporal clutched the arm of the woman on the floor and with my help pulled her up. She regained some composure and with a little physical encouragement we started moving her towards the shelter. The anti-aircraft guns opened up again and I knew the next wave would soon be on us.

"Come on!" I shouted and the three of us started to run.

The shelter was a brick building that had been set into the earth and covered in soil. At the entrance was a warrant officer. He grabbed the arms of both women and pushed them into shelter. I stopped short and looked back towards the airfield. There was little I could do, but I felt I didn't want to be too far away from the Hurricane.

"I need to look after that kite." I yelled at the warrant officer. As I stepped away he put a large hand on my shoulder and pulled me back.

"Don't try and be a bloody hero." He was a big man with a grim face. "There's bugger all you can do to save it now." With that he pushed me into the darkness of the shelter. Although I objected to the manhandling, I knew he was right.

Two benches ran down either side of the narrow shelter. Thick wooden struts held the roof in place and in the middle two oil lamps had been lit. The atmosphere was dank and cool compared to the dry dust of the trench. A cluster of anxious faces dimly lit by the oil lamps watched me. I sat down on the edge of a bench.

The first bomb from the second wave exploded. The panicked woman started whining again.

Crouching in the trench while the bombs fell had been terrifying, but in the shelter it was worse. While outside I could see what was going on and was free to move around. Here I felt trapped and I had no idea when the next bomb would explode. For several minutes we sat there while the bombs fell. One felt very close. My lungs tightened as the explosion sucked air out of the shelter. The two lamps flickered wildly in the draft.

I ran my fingers through my hair and dislodged a clump of soil. While I sat there I tried to analyse what was happening. Was this it? Had the Germans invaded? Being on the receiving end of the Stuka attack certainly felt as though they were close. Maybe Goering's plan had worked.

I lost count of how many bombs were dropped. Every explosion chipped away at my nerves until I could take it no more. I leapt up and ran out pushing past the warrant officer. I looked up to the sky, the last Stuka was heading back towards the coast and I could see no other attackers. The warrant officer joined me outside.

"Jesus Christ!" he whispered. Before us the landscape had been changed beyond recognition. It was almost as though we had been transported into an unfamiliar realm. We both stood still and looked on in astonishment.

Two of the large hangars had disappeared completely, the others were wrecked and twisted like a surrealist's painting. An intense fire raged amongst the rubble and thick black smoke rose up a thousand feet into the air. Leaves had been blown off the trees, the dry ground had been cracked and tiles had slid from the roofs leaving gaping holes. The atmosphere had become heavy with soot and smoke which formed a strange unnatural mist. An acrid smell of burning debris stung my nostrils and made my eyes water. All around a chalky white dust had settled like a snow flurry in spring. The infrastructure of the airfield which had taken years to build had been destroyed in a matter of ten minutes.

People began emerging from the shelters and trenches. There were yells and shouts as they started to search for survivors amongst the debris. I couldn't believe that anyone could have survived being in those buildings.

I was now convinced that the German invasion had started and it was my duty to get back to North Weald as quickly as possible. To my amazement I saw the Hurricane I was scheduled to fly still standing in one piece where I'd left it. I was fully expecting to find it shot up or damaged by bombs. I ran back to her and found the fuel bowser was also undamaged. It appeared the Stuka's main targets had been a group of aircraft over towards the western end of the airfield. These had all been reduced to indistinguishable piles of burning wreckage.

I gave the Hurricane a quick look over, running my hands over the wings and fuselage looking for any damage. Apart from being covered in dust it seemed fine. While standing on the wing I looked back at the devastated hangars. I could see a semblance of order was taking shape as the well drilled fire crews battled with the flames, and the medical teams attended the casualties. By one of the buildings I spotted the fitter who had been pouring coolant into the aircraft before the raid.

"You there!" I shouted. He looked round and I

beckoned him over with a wave of my hand. As he came towards me I noticed he was limping.

"You alright?" I asked.

"Twisted my bloody ankle running from a jerry bomb."

"Can you get that bowser going? I need to get this to North Weald."

"Alright. Stay there and I'll pass up the hose." He limped around to the bowser and set about starting the pumps. He came up to the aircraft holding the end of the hose with the nozzle.

"You know what you're doing up there?" he said as I searched around the wing root for the fuel filler.

"Where's the bloody cap?" I shouted.

"It's there, by your finger. You need to use the key that's tied to the hose."

After some fumbling I managed to undo the cap and set the nozzle into the tank. While the fuel was flowing I looked up at the sky. The grey smoke was still rising high above us and casting a murky shadow across the airfield. Two aircraft were approaching at low level. I froze for a moment worried that they were returning Stukas, but fortunately they were Hurricanes coming into land.

We filled up with forty gallons of fuel, enough to get me to North Weald if I flew a straight course. While the fitter moved the bowser I walked onto the runway to check if the ground was clear. The other Hurricanes seemed to have landed without any issue, but I could see two or three large craters I'd have to avoid. As I walked back I noticed the burned wreckage of another Hurricane, it looked like a pilot had struggled to land successfully.

I was almost ready to go, but I was missing a vital

piece of flying gear, I didn't have a parachute.

"Where can I get a parachute?" I asked the fitter.

"Well the stores was over there." He pointed to one of the flatten buildings. I snorted in frustration. I was so eager to get away from Tangmere, I didn't have the time to go searching for a parachute.

"Bugger it! I'll go without one." I was planning to fly low and quickly back to North Weald. If I ran into trouble I probably won't have the height to bail out. There was one issue though, the parachute pack formed a cushion when you sat on it. Without one I'd be too low in the seat.

"Get me something to sit on." I shouted at the fitter. He thought for a moment then ran off and returned a few seconds later with two sets of white cricket pads.

"Where the bloody hell did you get these?" I asked as we stuffed them into the cockpit.

"They were in the cab of the bowser. Lord knows why."

I climbed in and sat down. I was a little low in the seat, but it would have to do. I ran quickly through the cockpit checks. Everything appeared fine.

"Ready to give it a whirl then?" said the fitter. "Fingers crossed she's got enough battery." He smiled and jumped down. I took a deep breath and double checked the throttle and fuel cock. I had my fingers less than an inch from the starter when a face appeared at the cockpit side.

"What the hell do you think you're doing?" It was a red faced officer with squashed nostrils and dark eyes.

"I've got to get this to North Weald."

"She's not been signed off yet. The maintenance schedule is incomplete and you haven't got the form seven hundred."

I looked beyond him into the southern sky and checked once more for any incoming raiders.

"If you've got the paperwork I'll take it with me." I suggested.

"The file is in the hangar office."

"Where's that?" I asked.

We both looked across at the smouldering pile of bricks and timbers that had until recently been a hangar.

"Well when you find it at the bottom of that mess, send it to me at North Weald." I snapped as I reached forward and pressed the starter. The engine erupted into life and the officer was forced to slide down the wing and join the fitter who was standing by the tip. As I swung the aircraft round I glanced at the officer whose face had now turned a deeper shade of red. I admired that officer's devotion to his duty. Even under fire and the threat of invasion he was determined to ensure that all paperwork must be completed.

I gingerly moved out between the craters and onto a stretch of runway that was clear. I throttled forward and crossed my fingers, if anything was going to go wrong it was likely to happen on take off. The tail lifted and I was airborne, so far so good.

I banked round gently to the north and looked over the desolation below. From two hundred feet I could clearly see the damage that had been done. The towering column of smoke smudged and stained the fertile Sussex landscape. Eleven men lay dead amongst the wreckage.

I kept low and flew dead north. Back in the cockpit I felt much more relaxed. On the ground I'd been at the mercy of the enemy, up here I was in control, able to move freely and defend myself. I wasn't sure if the aircraft had been armed with ammunition. I pointed the nose down towards a vast cornfield and pressed the trigger. Nothing happened, either the guns didn't work or they'd not been loaded.

I searched around the horizon expecting to see smoke rising from other targets, but it all seemed strangely calm. High above me vapour trails criss crossed the deep blue atmosphere, someone was having a scrap up there. With limited fuel and no ammunition I was in no shape for a fight. I pressed on home, eventually crossing the Thames and reaching Essex. To my relief I found no fires raging at North Weald as I slipped into the landing pattern. In fact the airfield looked remarkably quiet in comparison to the chaos I'd left behind on the south coast. I taxied to the Dispersal Hut and shut down the engine.

"What the hell happened to you?" asked Aussie who was slumped in a deck chair. My trousers had been torn below the knee, my uniform was covered in dust and a yellow stain from the sandbags ran across my arm. At some point I'd received a cut above my eye. The blood had run down my face and dried on my cheek. In my hands I held the pair of cricket pads. I didn't have the energy to answer him.

The invasion wasn't under way as I'd assumed. Instead the Luftwaffe had targeted certain airfields and radar stations with huge numbers of bombers. I remembered Shelton's thoughts on not understanding the enemy tactic. It seemed now he was targeting the RAF stations on the ground.

That evening I stood in the shower washing more clumps of soil from my hair. I looked down at my naked form. It was gaunt and exhausted. The outside of my left knee was tender and a scab was forming where my leg had been pushing against the side of the cockpit. I felt I was being shaped to fit in a Hurricane in the same way a blacksmith hammers a bolt to fit a bracket.

Chapter 12
A letter

Dear Mother

Thank you for your last letter. I'm getting on well in the squadron. My fellow pilots are a great bunch of chaps and I've made lots of friends. We don't get out and about too much, but last week we went to the pictures and saw Rebecca.

Please let me know how father is getting along with the boat, I'm sure it won't be too long before we can go sailing again.

I've enclosed a picture of myself with a few of the boys here. On the left is Freddie and a Australian pilot we call Aussie. You can see I'm in the middle and on the right is my flight commander 'Mac' Mackay.

All my love
Jack

My letters home were pathetic. We never let our families know that we were in the thick of the fighting. Anyway the censor would bar us from divulging too much. Even if we had been able to tell those at home what we were facing, day in and day out, they'd never have understood. The battle had become very private to us.

My mother wrote to me every week with in-depth reports of my father's health and gossip from the parish. I replied when I could, in between flying, sleeping and drinking.

Chapter 13
Another letter.

HB relaxed behind his desk with his head half turned towards the window. Mac leant against the sill with his arms folded. Mabel lay on an old service blanket with her head resting on her paws. All three of them looked at me when I knocked on the open door.

"You wanted to see me sir?" I asked sheepishly.

"Come in," said HB sternly. I stepped into the small office and saluted. He looked up at me and then down onto the oak desk.

"What do you make of that?" He gestured towards a folded sheet of foolscap paper lying on the top in-tray. I hesitated for a moment and then picked it up. I could tell from the way the stiff paper was folded it was an official letter.

To: Squadron Leader Hardy Burton
Officer Commanding 506 Squadron, RAF North Weald

Dear Sir

On the 16th of August Hawker Hurricane VB765 was removed from Tangmere airfield by a sergeant pilot of 506 Squadron. Although the aircraft was scheduled to be sent to 506 Squadron, the correct paperwork was not in order.

I wish to bring a charge against the pilot who wilfully disobeyed my order not to take off. Please would you provide me with the name of the offending pilot and his current whereabouts. I also ask that you can provide me details of the current condition of the aircraft as we need to sign off our files at this end.

Yours Sincerely
Flt Lt D Fairhead
RAF Tangmere
Sussex

My eyes reached the bottom of the page and I looked up. I felt an anger swell as I picture that ruddy faced officer peering into the cockpit. HB was still looking out of the window.

"Tell me what happened down there," he said as I placed the paper back on the desk. I recounted what I did on that day. I saw no point in trying to cover up the fact that I'd disobeyed an order, besides I didn't want to lie to either HB or Mac. When I finished my account an uncomfortable silence fell upon the room. HB slowly rose from his chair and walked to the open door. I looked across at Mac, but he dropped his head to the floor and avoided my eyes.

"Palmer!" HB summoned the clerk from the next office where he was hammering the typewriter keys again. He bent down and stroked Mabel's head.

"Did you give your name to anyone there?" he enquired. I thought hard.

"No Sir, I don't think I did."

"Definitely?" probed Mac.

"Yes." I replied more assertively.

Palmer knocked on the door.

"Come in." said HB. "Take a letter please."

"Certainly Sir," replied Palmer as he produced a small notepad and pencil from his uniform pocket. He pulled up a spare chair and sat down at the side of the

HB's desk. HB stood up and started to pace the length of the room.

"To Flight Lieutenant Fairhead, RAF Tangmere." HB turned to check Palmer was ready to write and then continued.

"Thank you for your letter of the 17th August. With reference to your request for this pilot's name I would like to help you in this matter. However we have no record of which pilot that was. No doubt you appreciate that, like the rest of Fighter Command, 506 Squadron was extremely busy on the 16th of August and we had pilots and aircraft all over the South Coast. I would also like to help you with the information you requested about the Hurricane. Unfortunately, I believe the aircraft was shot down this morning and I feel it would be a waste of our resources to chase paperwork that relates to an aircraft which is currently at the bottom of the English Channel."

I looked out of the window where all the squadron aircraft were lined up. At the nearest end was the Hurricane that I'd brought back from Tangmere. I looked over at Mac and frowned in confusion. Mac shrugged his shoulders.

"Yours Sincerely, Squadron Leader Hardy Burton." HB finished the dictation and looked at Palmer who'd just finished scribbling on the pad.

"That'll get the buggers off the scent," quipped HB. Mac unfolded his arms and moved towards the door.

"Is that all sir?" he asked. HB nodded. I took the hint and walked towards the door, but stopped short and turned back.

"Thank you, sir," I said softly, but HB didn't react. Outside Mac smacked me on the shoulder.

"It sounded like you had a rough time at

Tangmere."

"It was terrifying. I was glad to get back in the air."
I looked towards the aircraft that had been the cause of
the problem.

"Why did he say it had been shot down?" I asked.

"Like he said, keep them off the scent," explained
Mac. "By the time anyone looks into the matter the
war will have moved on and God knows where we'll
be." He offered me a cigarette, I took one.

"Some people don't understand this damn war." He
went on. "These bloody pen pushers and civil servants,
they've got no idea what it's like up there. You know
that feeling that clutches your heart." He looked at me
with an intense expression. His eyes were bright and
wide but the skin around them sagged down to his
cheeks. He smiled and moved back slightly as though
he let his guard down too much.

"It's my birthday, so we're heading into Epping
tonight," he announced. "I plan to get completely
drunk."

Mac fulfilled his ambition that evening. By nine
o'clock a rambunctious celebration was well underway
in the public bar of the George. A few locals who'd
become familiar with our antics had joined us.
Fanshaw, the journalist, had arrived with a
sophisticated looking woman. Once again he took
turns with Warwick playing the piano, whilst Aussie
and Doc made concentrated advances on the barmaid.
She was however well experienced in fending off
drunken servicemen and kept them at bay. Toasts were
made in Mac's honour, which he gracefully received
and replied with an impromptu and mainly incoherent
speech. When the bell rang for last orders he was in no
fit state to drive, so I found myself behind the wheel of

his enormous green Bentley. I drove back carefully through the quiet lanes with Aussie sitting in the back and Mac slouched in the passenger's seat. Both were attempting to recite the words to a filthy limerick about a parson's daughter. I looked down the long bonnet and fixed my eyes on the white lines that marked the edge of the road. The steering was so heavy that turning a corner required a two handed manoeuvre several hundred feet before the junction. Somehow, we arrived back at the station in one piece and I parked as neatly as I could outside the Officers' Mess.

"You know it's a funny old war, Sommers," Mac slurred. "Has there ever been a time when a man goes into battle during the day and then in the evening gets pissed in the local pub?"

"Yeah, but it's still better than being on those bloody convoys," said Aussie. "Bobbing around in the middle of the Atlantic just waiting to be torpedoed. At least if we get shot down it'll be quick. Better than slowly drowning in icy cold water."

I left them in the car and navigated my way back to my room in a drunken stupor.

Chapter 14
The Red Devil

It was now obvious the Luftwaffe was attempting to destroy our airfields and radar stations. Through news reports and intelligence briefing we learnt about these attacks, and wondered when they would target us.

Two days after Mac's twenty sixth birthday, B-flight was tasked with another routine patrol of the Thames Estuary.

Flying in two sections we reached the River Medway and turned north east. The sky over England was clear. Across the North Sea cumulus clouds had formed like a distant mountain range. A strange dark hole had appeared in the middle of these brilliant white clouds. I studied it wondering what meteorological phenomenon had caused it.

Out of the corner of my eye something flashed passed me. I assumed it was the sun reflecting from my watch or maybe the glass in my goggles. But then I saw another flash, this time it was orange. Tracer! I checked the mirror. A swarm of Messerschmitt 109s were descending on us with guns blazing.

"Behind!" I screamed over the radio. I broke formation and pulled round hard to starboard. I had hoped to meet the fighters head on, but I had seen them too late and my reactions had been too slow. They were beyond me before I'd come around. I continued the turn until I'd passed through three hundred and sixty degrees. This had all taken valuable seconds, but I was now behind them and in a better position to try and attack.

Our formation was now in disarray. Yellow Section

had dived to port. One Hurricane was already belching out black smoke. I saw another was being pursued by two Messerschmitts. All three were turning tightly in a shallow dive. I rolled slightly and brought my nose into an angle that would converge on them. I was careful not to pick up too much speed and end up overshooting. They were a good fifteen hundred feet away and slightly below. On I flew. The cross hairs on my gunsight glowed orange, but I'd have to be much closer for a chance of hitting them.

I recognised the code letters on the Hurricane, it was Mac. He was in serious trouble, but managing to hold his aircraft in the turn as I came up from behind. I didn't see the lead Messerschmitt open fire, all I saw was a piece of debris separate from Mac's wing. A thousand feet, I was closer now, if Mac could just keep them in that position I could have a perfect shot. Annoyingly, the collar of my flying jacket had popped up from under my shoulder strap and was flapping around in the corner of my eye. Another piece flew up from Mac's wing. He turned tighter and I had to pull back to keep on the trajectory. Suddenly his canopy ripped away from the fuselage. I thought at first he might be about to bail out, but I didn't see a body emerge. Instead a sharp red flash came from the cockpit followed by a small orange glow which grew quickly into an intense fireball.

I was now in range, but I still couldn't turn hard enough to get a bead on either of the Messerschmitts. Then a large piece of Mac's port wing disintegrated and I watched in disbelief as the Hurricane flipped over on its back and began to spin. I looked for a parachute, but saw nothing other than the mass of metal, wood and flames spiralling to the ground.

"Mac! Get out!" I shouted over the radio. I thought I heard a faint click and muffled word, but that could have been any of the pilots.

The Messerschmitts, now seeing that their work was done, broke off and began to climb away.

As I watched them sprint into the wispy cloud a furious rage overcame me. I pushed the throttle open, pulled back the booster toggle and squeezed every bit of horsepower from the Merlin engine. I had one chance to hit them. I pulled back as hard as I could, until I was climbing vertically, but it was hopeless. I was unable to bring my guns to bear on either of them. They passed in front of me, but too high for me to attack. In the lead aircraft I could see the pilot with his black flying helmet and oxygen mask. He was staring straight ahead and oblivious to my presence. Painted on the fuselage, forward of the cockpit was a symbol, a cartoon devil encapsulated by a bright red circle. Beyond that was a black cross with its white outline and on the rudder was the sinister swastika.

To my frustration both aircraft pulled further and further away. They headed back out towards the sea and I knew they wouldn't stop until they were over the other side of the channel. Angrily I pushed the stick over and dived back towards where I'd come from. The sky was clear, the attackers had done their job well. They'd bounced us from the sun, done as much damage as possible and disappeared again. All within a matter of seconds.

With the dogfight dispersed I headed back to North Weald. I landed, shut down the engine and left the cockpit without saying a word to the ground crew.

I was the last pilot to arrive and the others were already huddled together outside the crew room discussing what had happened. I ripped my flying helmet off of my head and threw it on a chair. HB and the Adjutant had come out to see what was going on. The group was silent. HB looked inquiringly at me, aware that something wasn't right.

"We lost Mac," I snarled and turned my head away from his gaze.

"And Hill," added Freddie. I'd forgotten I'd seen a second Hurricane shot down.

Young men can easily become angry, adolescence is full of emotions that are difficult to understand and control. As I thought back to what had happened I was once again full of rage and as if possessed by an invisible spirit I lashed out with my boot and sent the wooden chair in front of me into the air. It came down on the hard ground and broke in two. I grunted through gritted teeth, fully aware that everyone was looking at me.

"Sommers. My office now," ordered HB. Like a petulant child expecting a scolding I followed him into the building.

"Close the door and sit down," he said calmly. He perched himself on the corner of his desk and pulled a packet of Dunhill from his pocket. He offered me one of the cigarettes and took one himself.

"What happened up there?" he asked. I took a long drag on the cigarette and then relayed everything that had happened. I must have spoken for a good five minutes, HB didn't interrupt, he just listened. I was candid about my actions and admitted we hadn't seen the Messerschmitts until the last minute. I questioned whether I should have stayed with Mac or maybe I should have tried to open fire from a longer range. When I stopped talking I looked at him expecting to see some form of emotion, but he was deadpan. I couldn't understand why he wasn't as upset as I was. After all, he'd known Mac a lot longer than I had.

He stood up from the desk and walked over to the wooden filing cabinet. Like a cliched scene from a Hollywood gangster movie he pulled out a bottle of whisky and two enamel cups from the top draw. As he poured two shots he spoke.

"The first pilot I lost on this squadron was called Mathews, he was a close friend of mine, we'd been at school together." He screwed the cap back on to the bottle. "I watched three 109s beat him up and he hit the ground in a field near Reims. You know I was so furious I chased them back over the German lines. In the end I nearly ran out of fuel and only just made it back over our own front." He handed me a drink.

Whisky doesn't look nearly as appealing in a chipped enamel cup as it does in a cut glass tumbler. I took a sip and the neat spirit made my body stiffen.

"Mac was a good officer and a good pilot." HB continued. "If he's dead there's nothing you can do about it." He took a sip himself. "It's all right to be angry, but don't get angry down here. Get angry up there with those bastards." He pointed his finger skywards.

"Finish your drink and clean yourself up. I need you back in the air this afternoon."

His last remark felt like having a bucket of icy cold water thrown in my face. I downed the whisky and handed him back the cup.

Everything changed on that day. Before I was a young man, barely out of puberty, insecure and introverted. The war was just a big adventure. Now, I felt I'd aged a decade in a day. I had witnessed a comrade killed, not in some obscure corner of the world, but over his own home county, in fact the burnt wreckage of his aircraft landed less than six miles from his parent's house.

I unbuttoned my tunic and threw it on the back of the chair. I put on my Mae West and sat down, tight lipped and angry. The rest of the pilots sat around as we always did, but that afternoon no one said a word. I stared at the open cockpit of my aircraft, the bright sun flared on the polished Perspex. I yearned for the shrill ring of the crew room telephone and the call to scramble. I wanted to be airborne, to fight, to avenge Mac's death.

A call did come through, about an hour later and I sprinted forward full of fury. The patrol however, was fruitless. We were directed over the North Sea, but no contact with the enemy was made. By the time we were stood-down my anger had begun to ebb away, but I was feeling restless.

That evening Freddie and I headed into Epping to relieve the tension. Somehow he'd managed to get a message through to Joan and Ada and they met us on the High Street. I'm still ashamed of what happened that evening. I drank far too much and behaved disgracefully. We visited a quiet pub on Half Moon Lane. I wanted to avoid the George and the memory of Mac's birthday. After a number of drinks I insisted that Ada and I went for a walk. We found a secluded alleyway by a butcher's shop. It all started with giggles and smiles as we started to explore each other. My hand ran down her side and over her hip. I pushed my fingers in between the top of her skirt and her warm flesh. Then I seemed to be overcome by some primal instinct which she did nothing to fend off. Judging by

the way she negotiated the fastenings on my uniform
and the speed at which things happened I don't think I
was the first serviceman she'd entertained in that
alleyway. It was a disappointing experience which left
me feeling empty. I returned to North Weald full of
alcohol and self-loathing. Back in my room I placed
my flying jacket on the bed and with a pen knife
started to cut away the collar.

Chapter 15
Formation Flying

The cast iron kettle vibrated on the pot belly stove and small clouds of steam coughed from the spout. The corporal wrapped an oil-stained rag around the handle and lifted it away. In front of a neat formation of tin mugs he poured the boiling water into a large teapot. Despite a few jocular remarks the atmosphere in the crew room was gloomy.

We watched the Adjutant as he wiped a damp cloth over the blackboard and Mac's name was erased from the squadron roster. With a fresh piece of white chalk he began to write in the space below the title Flight Commander: B-flight. Like a punctured tyre Freddie let out a long sigh when he saw Cavendish's name had appeared. I managed to restrain any verbal expressions although I felt my own body deflate as well. My own name remained on the blackboard as Yellow Two. I was now Cavendish's wingman. Low murmurs and mutterings bounced around the room. The Adjutant, well aware of the unpopular decision, promptly left to avoid any awkward questions.

"Suppose it was inevitable," muttered Freddie in a hushed tone. "Behind Mac he is the most senior officer."

"Well at least if he's in command of a flight he won't be able to give HB much grief." I tried to find a positive angle on the appointment.

"True, but now he's going to give us grief," Freddie remarked.

I took myself outside and lit a Craven A. I felt sick, I always felt sick. I had little appetite and most of my nutrients now came from a hip flask of cheap brandy I'd taken to carrying around. I looked back at the Dispersal Hut with its wooden walls being bleached in the sunlight and the moss growing on the roof. Where our feet had beaten down the grass, narrow tracks of compacted soil ran from the doorway to the aircraft. Nothing had changed physically, but it seemed such a different place from when I'd arrived three weeks ago as a freshly trained, and nervous pilot.

At the far end of the hut was Mac's Bentley still sitting where he'd left it the day before. With its large headlights the car looked sorrowful, like a faithful gundog waiting for its master to return. I walked over and ran my hand over the front wing disturbing a thin layer of dust which had settled in the dry weather.

"Flight Lieutenant Cavendish's compliments, Sarge." I spun around to find the duty corporal standing behind me.

"He'd like to have all the pilots of B-flight to assemble in the crew room in 10 minutes." It seemed ridiculously formal, like the kind of message a Napoleonic Captain would send to his First Lieutenant.

Cavendish waited until we were all sitting in the crew room before he entered. He strode between the chairs wearing his pristine flying suit like a head teacher about to address a school assembly.

"Gentlemen, I appreciate the last few days have been difficult," he spoke with his hands on his hips. "But it's now time for us to tidy up our flying skills and bring back some discipline into the squadron." Unable to concentrate on his presentation I found myself gazing at particles of dust as they sparkled in a ray of sunlight which cut across the room.

"Firstly we will tighten up our formations."
Cavendish continued.

"We will keep flying in two vees, but we will
dispense with having a weaver." To this instruction
there was a palpable sense of opposition. Most pilots
felt the tight vee formation was obsolete and preferred
to fly a looser configuration which allowed much more
opportunity to spot the enemy. The weaver was a
nominated pilot who would fly a zig zag pattern
behind the flight. He was there to protect our
vulnerable rear.

"So if we have no weaver, how the hell do we keep
an eye out behind?" asked Doc. Being an officer he
was in a stronger position to challenge the proposed
strategy. Cavendish however ignored the remark and
spoke again.

"I also want to review our take off procedure." He
took his hands from his hips and started to point with
his fingers. "In future I want to ensure that my aircraft
is the first airborne with the rest of my section
following and then Red Section."

"So you want us to perform a formation take off?"
Doc piped up again with an air of insubordination.

"Yes." Cavendish replied firmly.

"Even when we're scrambled?" Doc asked.

"Yes! Even when we're scrambled." Came another
firm reply. A variety of frowns and grimaces appeared
on our faces. It had been impressed on all squadrons
that when scrambled we had to get airborne as soon as
possible. Cavendish was now telling us we had to wait
until he was trundling down the runway before we
could open up the throttle. This made no sense. If his
aircraft or any in front failed to start, which often
happened, we'd have to twiddle our thumbs until he

was ready. All of this could cost valuable seconds and most probably minutes.

Doc went to speak again, but this time Cavendish cut him short.

"We will be standing-to in half an hour. Ensure you are ready." With that he left the room.

We patrolled later that morning and gave the residents of Harwich a demonstration of close formation flying, but made no contact with the enemy.

An hour after landing we were scrambled to intercept a formation of bombers crossing the North Sea. Although no conspiracy had been planned it appeared every pilot in B-flight made an extra effort to get their machine airborne quickly. As a result Cavendish was the last pilot in the air. He was furious when we landed and threatened to put us all on a charge. We let him vent his anger knowing full well he had no case against us. The orders from Group were to get airborne as quickly as possible and that's what we had done.

Strangely Cavendish's fractious style of management had a cohesive effect on us. Within the squadron he had always been socially awkward, but now he was in a position of authority, those under his command bonded together rather like prisoners beneath the watchful gaze of a warden.

I suppose it was puerile, but I found our game of annoying Cavendish was a welcome distraction. HB was well aware of our antics and as long as we didn't overstep the mark he didn't interfere.

I found a stranger in my room that evening. He was lying asleep in shirt sleeves on top of Lanky's bed. He woke when I closed the door and sat bolt upright. He was short in stature, had a broad face, prominent cheekbones and piercing blue eyes.

"Hello." I greeted him. "I take it you're my new roommate?"

He smiled awkwardly and spoke in broken English.

"I am Jakub Vaclav." I looked over at his tunic which was hung neatly on the wardrobe. Above the three sergeant's chevrons the word Czechoslovakia was sewn.

"You're Czech?" I asked. He looked confused so I repeated the question and gestured to my own shoulder. This time he understood.

"Yes, I join 506 Squadron." I looked back at his uniform. On the breast was an ornate badge. A silver wreath set under a pair of golden wings, the Czech pilot insignia. Above the uniform on top of the wardrobe was a battered blue violin case.

Later I discovered Jakub was not the only new pilot. Another Czech by the name of Tomáš Novák and an officer called Davis had arrived. Davis had been with the squadron in France but had injured himself in a landing accident. He'd spent several weeks in hospital and was once again fit for flying.

It was an awkward evening, the Czechs seemed apprehensive and the language barrier made things all the worse. I opted for an early bed but found it difficult to sleep in such a sober state.

Much to their bemusement, the Czechs were not on the flying roster the following morning. They were keen to get flying and fighting, just like I had been all those weeks ago. There appeared to be some hesitation in allowing these foreign pilots near our machines and HB insisted they wouldn't be allowed up until he'd checked them out personally. I tried to console them by explaining I'd had the same restrictions, but they believed they were being side-lined. I couldn't blame them as they had already been the butt of a number of prejudiced jokes and comments.

Chapter 16
The Fighting Refugees

The great air battle which has been in progress over this Island for the last few weeks has recently attained a high intensity. It is too soon to attempt to assign limits either to its scale or to its duration. We must certainly expect that greater efforts will be made by the enemy than any he has so far put forth.

Winston Churchill to the House of Commons 20th of August 1940

After a week of strict regimented flying we'd settled into Cavendish's leadership, although it had produced no results.

Time had become difficult to measure. The days seem to pass quickly and yet the month appeared never ending. The weather was indecisive, dazzling us with warm sunshine one minute and then miserable drizzle the next. The unpredictable climate curtailed the enemy's plans and gave us a very brief respite.

With little else to do we played game upon game of Gin Rummy; we had lost our cricket ball when Warwick drove it deep into a distance patch of brambles. The card games had given me a chance to know the Czechs a little better. To relieve his boredom Jakub started to practice his violin in the Dispersal Hut, much to Aussie's irritation. The two Eastern Europeans were incredibly polite, but their patience was wearing thin, days had passed and they still weren't operational.

One afternoon a break in the cloud appeared and

HB seized the opportunity to test their skills.

He leapt into the crew room with a burst of enthusiasm.

"Alright get your kit together and let's see what you chaps can do."

Cavendish scoffed from behind a book as the two pilots jumped to their feet.

"Err which machine do we take?" Tomáš asked. His accent always carried an apologetic tone. HB looked out of the window at the line of Hurricanes.

"Sommers, how's your kite holding up?" He threw me a look which demanded an honest answer.

"She was fine this morning Sir," I said folding up a well-read copy of the Telegraph.

"Novák, take Warwick's aircraft and Vaclav, you take Sommer's kite."

Jakub looked at me.

"Thank you."

"Just bring her back in one piece," I replied, mimicking the stern warning Aussie had given me when I borrowed his Hurricane.

Outside, the sun had burnt through the cloud and bathed the airfield in a vibrant light while a dark grey skyline rolled on to the South. Aussie was leaning against the doorframe watching HB give one of his thorough briefings to the two Czechs. I pulled out a packet of Craven A and offered him one.

"You reckon they'll do all right?" I asked.

"Don't underestimate them. They've done a lot more flying than some of us." He took a Swan Vesta box from his pocket and without looking struck a match across the coarse sandpaper.

"Trouble is, His Majesty's Royal Air Force can be an awkward place if you don't have the right accent. I know that only too well." He lit the cigarette.

"I don't think it's just the accent," I remarked. "If you didn't go to the right school and your father was a tradesman you've got no chance." Aussie looked at me.

"What did your old man do then?"

"Served his time as a carpenter, then became a timber merchant. He did all right. Made enough to give us a good education and a happy childhood, but there's no noble blood in our family."

"Christ, I'm surprised they let you through the main gates." Aussie laughed and took another drag.

The Merlin engines came to life and produced a deep throated harmony that resonated around the wooden buildings. They started to move down the runway. Jakub was a little sharp on the brakes, but every aircraft is different and it always takes a pilot time to adjust. They moved slowly at first but then faster and faster. Almost in unison each empennage lifted like a mare's tails in a dressage display. Gently the three aircraft rose into the sky. By now they were some distance from us, but we could see the undercarriage retract and tuck neatly away. It was a tricky business to operate the throttle, control column and undercarriage lever at the same time and I fully expected to see the Czechs struggle to keep the aircraft straight and level, but both flew on without issue.

"Good take off," said Aussie softly.

Both Jakub and Tomáš were very experienced pilots. Jakub had been born not far from Prague. His mother was a Russian Jew and his father a Bohemian. Both were musicians who met in an orchestra, hence the violin case which appeared on top of our wardrobe. Jabuk had joined the Czech air force not long before

Hitler annexed the Sudetenland, which in turn led to the occupation of the rest of his country. At the time I was ignorant of what was happening to Jews under the Nazi regime. When Jakub described the atrocities of the Kristallnacht and why he had felt so threatened I found it hard to believe such events could happen in modern Europe.

He had managed to avoid capture and made his way to Poland where he joined the Polish Air Force. This was where he met his fellow countryman Tomáš and the two pilots were sent to an airfield near Warsaw. For three weeks they flew and fought as best they could, but the Luftwaffe had a far greater strength and superior machines. When their airfield was close to being overrun the two men managed to escape. They found passage on a ship and after several days at sea made it to the Netherlands. From there they crossed into France and volunteered for the Armée de l'Air. They were treated with an air of suspicion by the French authorities, who were already beset by many problems and didn't have the resources to assess the large groups of refugee pilots who were arriving daily. Eventually they were assigned to a unit flying Bloch MB150s, an aircraft outclassed on all levels by the German 109.

France fell a matter of days later and the two men once again found themselves running from the German army. In a matter of months they had fought in three different countries and finally found themselves in England. They arrived in Dover with nothing except their threadbare uniforms and Jakub's violin. Despite their keenness there were reservations about them joining the RAF. Concerns were raised over the language barrier and whether they would fall in line with the disciplines. By July 1940 there was a desperate shortage of aircrew and the RAF started to integrate the hundreds of Eastern European pilots who ended up exiled in England.

Aussie walked back inside and found an enamel mug. He ran a finger around the inside to remove a line of scum left by the last beverage. He looked over towards Cavendish who was sitting reading his book.

"You know I'd rather have one of those guys on my wing than some of the senior pilots in this goddamn outfit," whispered Aussie just loud enough for me to hear.

"Never underestimate the strength of man fighting for his homeland," he remarked as though he was quoting Shakespeare. I was tempted to point out that most of us in the squadron were currently fighting for our own homeland, but I thought better of it. After years of nomadic employment I don't think he knew exactly where he belonged.

Sometime later the familiar drone of the Hurricanes drifted over the airfield. I looked over to see the three aircraft passing to the west in tidy formation. They ran directly over the airfield and neatly broke formation like a troupe of well rehearsed chorus girls. A few of the other pilots had also come out to watch. A true indication of a pilot's skill is landing and we were all curious to see how the Czechs got on.

There was a slight crosswind blowing across the airfield, but both pilots made allowance for this with a small amount of rudder. I felt apprehensive, I was obviously concerned for Jakub safety, but I'd grown so fond of that Hurricane I didn't want to see it smashed into the deck. I thought Jakub was a little too high, but I was wrong, all three aircraft touched down in perfect three point landings and none of them bumped back into the air, a trait I was often guilty of. The aircraft all parked neatly and the ever-loyal ground crew scampered out to attend. HB sprang from his cockpit in his usual energetic style. He gathered the two pilots together and I saw him gesturing with his hands to demonstrate some point about the formation they'd just flown. Mabel shot out of the office and bounded towards her master. HB finished his debrief and walked back into the crew room.

"Get them on the duty roster for tomorrow." I heard him say as he passed the Adjutant.

. . .

I felt sick, horrendously sick. I needed fresh air so I slid back the canopy and pulled the tight fitting oxygen mask away from my face. The compass said I was heading north east which surprised me as I thought I was heading due South. I had passed out. We'd engaged an enormous formation of bombers off Ramsgate. It was a furious dogfight and I remembered pulling up hard and trying to get behind a 109, but that was all. I could only assume I'd exerted so much G force I'd lost consciousness and let go of the controls. I'd never passed out before. The experience seemed to last for hours, but it must have only been seconds. I remembered a hazy feeling and my body refusing to move. When I came to the aircraft had corrected itself, but alarmingly I'd descended by six thousand feet. The sparkling sea was now only nine hundred feet below. Thank God I'd not passed out at a lower altitude or I'd have hit the waves.

I banked into a gentle turn, I was still disoriented and for all I knew I could have been flying over the Bay of Bengal, reassuringly though the Kent coastline came into view. Thousands of feet above a criss-cross of vapour trails hung where the fighting had taken place. I felt weak, but I knew I must climb back up into the thick of it. I pushed the throttle forward and headed upwards. The fighting was over by the time I arrived and the vapour trails had faded into the atmosphere. I ambled around in the empty air and saw some aircraft in the far distance. They were heading back out to sea. My stomach was still unsettled so I decided to head back home, disappointed with my efforts.

About six miles out I spotted the smoke. A great black flurry rising high and leaning with the wind. I'd seen a sight like that before, at Tangmere after the dive bombing. Now my own station had been assaulted.

I searched the sky to see if the attackers were still there. Then I flew a wide circuit around the perimeter like a bird protecting its nest. The Luftwaffe had long since left, after dropping nearly two hundred bombs. From the air I could see the station was in disarray and a line of pot marks and craters ran across the airfield and on the Ongar Road.

The runway looked undamaged and I could see a Hurricane landing while another was taxing up to our end of the field. I assumed it was safe to come in and did so. I passed over the smoke and I felt the aircraft jolt as the heat of the fire swelled up underneath. Once down I taxied up towards the Dispersal Hut and shut down the engine. I fully expected one of the ground crew to appear, but no-one did. After making the aircraft safe I undid my straps and stood up. Warwick stood by my wingtip.

"Looks like the Mary Celeste round here," he said with a concerned frown.

"Where is everyone?" I asked.

"Beats me, but it looks like we took a pasting." He gestured towards the smoke. Freddie stood up in the cockpit of the other Hurricane.

"What a bloody mess." He looked across the airfield. "Where are the erks?"

"We don't know." I shrugged.

"Jesus Christ what's that?" Warwick pointed to the plump figure of the Adjutant who was jogging towards us. He was wearing a tin helmet with one arm clamped on top. Even at a distance we could see his face was a brighter red than usual.

"Diverted!" He shouted with a wave of his free arm. He stopped at my tailplane and bent forward. Large patches of sweat had formed around his armpits. I thought he was just about to collapse.

"They've been," he caught his breath "they've been diverted. The squadron's gone to Hornchurch." He coughed up a foul sound from deep within his lungs. "You should have heard it on the radio." We all looked at each other blankly.

"What happened here?" asked Freddie.

"They hit us about thirty minutes ago." The Adjutant had regained a little composure.

"They missed the airfield, but hit the station. The Officers' Mess and a few other buildings. One of the shelters took a direct hit."

"Shall we get over to Hornchurch?" asked Freddie.

"I'll try and get word to them, but now you're here you're probably better off staying."

155

The ground crew had been seconded to help with the bomb damage. We needed to refuel and re-arm our aircraft so the Adjutant managed to retrieve Edwards and a fuel bowser. With no other ground crew available, Warwick and I set to refuelling the aircraft, while Freddie and Edwards started to re-arm the machine guns. We took far longer on both jobs than the well practiced erks did and my admiration for the ground crews grew tenfold. Mabel patrolled back and forth outside the Dispersal Hut keeping watch for more enemy raiders.

The squadron returned from Hornchurch in the early evening, by which time the station was operational again. That evening as Freddie and I walked back to the billet we surveyed the damage done by the raiders. A section of the Officer's Mess was destroyed. Wisps of smoke drifted up from the debris and mixed with the drizzle creating thin bands of smog. Splinters of wood and buckled steel protruded from the rubble. Civilian labourers were picking through the wreckage. Damage teams always worked silently, constantly listening for sounds of trapped survivors. Two men were pulling out an iron bedstead while another salvaged clothes and uniform from an upturned wardrobe. Across the road stood a large oak tree. Its thick trunk and wide boughs suggested it had been growing on that verge well before someone had built an airfield here. A great strip of bark lay by its roots. It had been torn from the trunk leaving a deep scar in the flesh of the tree. Every building close by had lost its windows in the blast. The facades looked like a gallery of morose faces with blackened eyes. A few personal items from those who had been killed were piled on the grass. I felt ashamed that we'd not been able to protect them.

The same acrid smell of charred wood and burnt tar that I'd smelt at Tangmere lingered in the air. It spread throughout the station and permeated my own bedroom. I lay there that night unable to sleep. The smell dredged up terrible images from deep within my mind.

Chapter 17
Radio Silence

The following day was colder, but clearer. The sun was now rising later in the day which allowed a few more precious minutes in bed.

My logbook now boasted sixty operational sorties. On nearly half of these I had had contact with the enemy. I was no longer considered a novice fighter pilot.

The squadron had crystallised as a fighting unit. Scrambles and patrols were second nature, but for all this the fear had not left me, in fact it had grown. Any distraction which prevented me from thinking too deeply was welcomed.

In the late morning the whole squadron was scheduled to patrol. We had just got airborne when Aunty directed us towards a group of raiders.

I'd taken to flying with my canopy slightly open. The rush of air made the stuffy cockpit more bearable as a noxious odour of high-octane fuel had been developing over the last few days. Edwards suspected a leaking pipe somewhere behind the bulkhead, but as of yet he had not been able to fix the issue. A layer of wispy cloud appeared to hang motionless in the tranquil sapphire sky. The sun glinted off my wing where the paint had worn thin and the bare metal was exposed. I was tucked in neatly beside Cavendish's aircraft. In front, and slightly lower, HB was leading A-flight. We'd risen above the layer of cloud in search of our quarry, which some keen observer on the ground had spotted heading towards Canvey Island. My eyes flicked between my instrument panel and the rest of the formation.

In my drafty cockpit an uneasy feeling crept over me, I knew something was wrong. I gently moved the control column from side to side. The aircraft was handling fine, the engine was running sweetly, but I felt unbalanced. Then it dawned on me, there was no sound in my headphones. While the radio was on the set constantly emitted a low hum. I caught hold of the cable which ran from my helmet and made sure it was connected to the set. It was, so I pulled the plug out and pushed it back in firmly. Still no sound. I pressed the transmit button and spoke.

"Panther leader, Yellow two radio check." I waited, there was no reply. Having no radio communication made me feel very vulnerable. An order could be given to climb or break at any moment and I would be none the wiser. This meant I could be in the wrong position and in danger of colliding with another aircraft. I used a little stick to slip away from Cavendish and gave myself some space. I fiddled again with the radio control, but no amount of switching or clicking would bring it to life. In frustration I resorted to thumping the box, which in a confined space was difficult. Still nothing. I resigned myself to being the custodian of a dead radio set.

By now a large gap had grown between myself and Cavendish. I decided the best thing to do was fall behind the formation where there would be less chance of collision. I waved my wings to attract Cavendish's attention, but he was staring dead ahead, oblivious to the other aircraft around him. Then I eased the throttle back slightly and let the flight move away from me. I let a good five hundred feet grow between us and just for luck gave the radio transmitter another thump. Still no sound in my headphones.

Below, the cloud had started to thin and I could see the coastline. Just in front of my starboard wing a reflection of the sun flashed and sparkled. You often see these flashes from such an altitude, usually it's light bouncing off of water or large areas of glass like a greenhouse. This flash seemed different. I banked the wing slightly and saw below me the dark green shape of a Junkers 88 bomber passing underneath the cloud. It was the angular transparent canopy, not dissimilar to a greenhouse that had reflected the sun. It was most probably the aircraft we'd been dispatched to intercept. I had to act quickly. The rest of the squadron was now a fair distance from me. By the time I tried to re-join them and communicate with hand signals the bomber could be lost in the cloud.

"Bugger!" I swore to myself. Once more I pressed the Bakelite button on the radio in the vain hope I'd transmit something.

"Tally Ho! Yellow Two. Below six o'clock," but the airwaves remained silent. I waggled my wings violently in case one of the other pilots saw me and then I banked over into a shallow dive. Maybe if the squadron noticed I was missing they might follow.

Immediately I was descending through the cloud. Cloud is a real danger to aviators. The mesmerising white vapour engulfs the canopy and obscures any visual reference. It's all too easy to become disoriented as the different forces pull and push your body. In these circumstances even experienced pilots have been known to stall or end up flying upside down when they were convinced they were straight and level.

I kept a careful watch on my instruments as the world outside became a white fog. Then slowly the cloud thinned and the earth appeared below.

More by luck than judgement I broke through above and behind the Junkers 88. He was not alone, another three flew in tight formation. I pulled the stick back and levelled off keeping within the very bottom of the cloud base. This way I could hide while I planned my attack.

The Junkers 88 was a fast twin-engine bomber. Its crew of four all sat in the compact cockpit which bristled with seven point nine two calibre machine guns. Its main defence however was its speed.

With a gentle bank I brought myself over to the portside of the enemy formation. I was still scraping the clouds and doing my best to hide above the bombers. I looked over both shoulders, no sign of the squadron, I was on my own. I had two thousand four hundred rounds of ammunition between my eight browning machine guns. That gave me around sixteen seconds of firing. I knew the moment I started my attack the formation would break up and try to evade me.

The little orange crosshair flickered as I switched on the gunsight. With my left thumb and forefinger I twisted the brass ring on the control column and set the guns to the fire position. Very gently I lowered the nose and banked to starboard, this brought me into position for a beam attack on the nearest aircraft. I aimed at the port engine and cockpit of the bomber. I throttled back slightly to compensate for the momentum I was gaining in the dive. The dark shape grew larger in my sight.

I fully expected a volley of tracer to come racing towards me from one of the twelve machine guns, but the cloud had hidden me well and the element of surprise was still mine. I could clearly see the pilot and his crew moving around the cockpit.

At three hundred feet I pressed the gun button. I held it for maybe two seconds. The familiar vibration from the Brownings shook through the aircraft. Almost immediately I passed over the bomber without seeing if my volley had been successful. My attack now brought me inline with the middle aircraft, but my speed was too great to allow a decent shot. Instead another few degrees of bank allowed me a better chance on the starboard most aircraft.

This time I was slightly head on to his port quarter. His forward machine gun came to life and then came the tracer that I had been expecting. I answered with another two second burst of gunfire straight into the cockpit. I saw some debris fly up from my shots, but again I was over and gone before I could see if I'd done any real damage. After passing by I turned in a wide arc to bring myself behind the formation, or what remained of it. With a quick glance I saw one of the 88s peeling off to the left in a very steep dive. On the other side, the aircraft I'd just attacked was plummeting to earth.

From its starboard wing a thin line of dark smoke streamed out. The black line stained the sky tracing the route of the aircraft's descent. I'd lost sight of the middle aircraft, but the formation leader was still flying straight and level about fifteen hundred feet ahead. I pushed the throttle forward and raced towards him. His gunner spotted me from a fair distance and started firing. I weaved sharply to make his job more difficult. The Junkers broke to the left, but I'd anticipated the move and followed him round. I was now in perfect range, but we were turning hard. I pulled around tighter to bring my aim in front of the bomber. This was known as a deflection shot, much like trying to hit a duck with a shotgun. You need to compensate for the speed and angle by aiming in front.

I pressed the gun button. My aim was too shallow and I missed him. I pulled tighter still bringing my aim even further in front. I fire again. This time I saw something break away from the bomber as my bullets hit. Confident that I had my eye in, I continued firing. This time a long burst. More debris parted from the aircraft and a vivid orange flame streaked out of the port engine. I gave another burst and my guns stopped, my ammunition was spent.

The Junkers adopted a peculiar attitude moving sideways with its nose raised. I could see why. I'd hit the starboard wing and the aileron, which was vital to controlling the aircraft, had disintegrated. The pilot was now battling to keep the machine airborne. I climbed a little to lose some speed and watched the forlorn aircraft slipping out of control. It seemed to hang in the air and I judged it must have been very close to stalling.

I lost sight of it for a few seconds as I circled around. When it came back into view it was performing a slow cartwheel. One after the other, two beige coloured blobs shot out of the cockpit. A stream of white silk ripped from their backs and two of the crew drifted down under the canopies of their parachutes. I continued to circle, fascinated by the spectacle. I knew there should be four men in that aircraft, but only two parachutes appeared. The aircraft continued to fall slowly, turning end on end until it sank into a vertical dive. I raced down and watched as the ten ton German bomber smashed into the centre of a large wheat field. The explosion was short and sharp, sending a ball of flame into the air. The vivid fire and grey smoke left an ugly scar on a landscape that could have inspired Elgar. I passed overhead as people from the nearby village came out to see what had happened. I waggled my wings over a school yard where a group of children stood looking skywards and I headed back to North Weald.

It was something of an anti-climax arriving at the airfield. As I shut down the big Merlin and the propeller came to a stop the whole aircraft seemed to sigh. I took off my leather helmet and undid the canvas shoulder straps. All around was quiet, save for the few birds who sang in a distant hedgerow. The aircraft rocked as someone jumped on to the wing. The ever reliable face of Flight Sergeant Edwards loomed above the cockpit.

"All good in there lad?" he asked.

"Just about," I panted. Edwards looked down at the shredded red canvas gun covers and the fresh lines of black cordite that streaked across the wing. A sure sign that my guns had fired.

"Run into some Jerries up there?" he enquired.

"Four of the buggers."

With my straps now undone I was able to lean forward and inspect the radio set.

"Damn thing gave up on me." I pulled out the headset plug.

"Okay, I'll get the sparks over." Edwards said as he cupped his hands into the shape of a megaphone and shouted towards a group of men by the huts.

"Wilson! Over here at the double and bring your tool kit."

I climbed out and slung my parachute over the tail

plane. I ran my fingers through my hair in an effort to look more presentable. At the Dispersal Hut I found my hip flask hidden in my jacket. I unscrewed the silver-plated cap and breathed in the sweet and woody aroma. I raised the flask and pursed my lips. The familiar sting made my tongue tingle and I winced. Then followed that warm glow which spread across my chest and into my lungs. I felt my muscles relax and the world seemed to revolve a little slower. I lit a Craven A from a crumpled packet and walked back outside.

As I looked over the quiet airfield I started to realise the magnitude of what had just happened. Even fresh in my own memory it appeared far fetched. How was I going to put this in a combat report without sounding like I was spinning a yarn?

The squadron returned about forty minutes later and a little while after that I found myself summoned to the CO's office. Just as before HB sat behind his desk while Mabel lay half asleep in her bed. But this time instead of Mac's gangly figure propped casually against the windowsill Cavendish stood glaring at me from behind HB. Shelton the intelligence officer was also present, sitting at the end of the desk fingering a stack of combat reports.

HB used his forefinger to loosen his collar and lent back in his chair.

"This is quite a claim." He nodded towards the papers. "One Ju 88 and two probables from a solo attack?" His eyes locked on mine. "What happened up there?" Seeing as I'd already given a full report to Shelton I felt this was a polite way of saying we don't believe you.

"I'm afraid my radio failed and rather than risk

colliding with…."

"Utter rubbish!" Cavendish cut me short. I took a deep breath and rocked back on to my heels.

"I'm sorry sir, but my radio was failing to transmit or receive."

"No I'll tell you what happened!" Cavendish jabbed the air with his finger. "You saw Jerry and thought you'd slip off and have a crack at them all on your own."

I bit down on my bottom lip and tried to quash the angry rage which was swelling inside me. HB raised an open hand in the space between myself and Cavendish.

"I would like Sommers to give his own account." He sounded like a high court judge.

I took another breath and began to recount what had happened once more. When I finished HB looked towards Shelton who'd been making notes on a sheet of paper. He spoke over his thick round spectacles.

"It's a remarkable piece of flying, if true. No doubt we'll find some evidence to prove or disprove the story."

His words rekindled the anger inside me. I felt like an innocent man being accused of some heinous crime. I'd carried out my duty to the utmost only to be doubted by my superiors. There was a knock at the door.

"Come in," said HB

Edwards in his oil stained overalls marched in and saluted.

"All the aircraft have been checked over and made ready sir." He brought up a clipboard from his left hand to read the reports. "All aircraft are serviceable, but two aircraft due for engine changes and another is due for an airframe inspection." He tucked the clipboard back under arm.

"And Sommers' Hurricane? What happened with the radio?" asked HB. Edwards looked back at his clipboard.

"The set had shorted out. The electrician has replaced the fuse and he's testing it now."

I breathed a sigh of relief, thank God the set had been faulty and it wasn't just finger trouble on my part.

"Well gentlemen, that proves part of the story," HB said with a slight air of relief.

"That may be the case, but I don't swallow this three kill claim." Cavendish stared at me while he spoke. I stared back at him. Any fragments of respect I had for this man had completely evaporated.

"Time will tell," HB said philosophically. He rose to his feet and walked to the window where he surveyed the cloud formation. "Thank you gentlemen, that will be all."

News of my claim had already circulated amongst the other pilots and when I walked outside I was mobbed with more questions. I did discover my attempt to alert the other aircraft about the Ju 88s had not gone unnoticed. All of the aircraft of Red Section saw what I was up to and called Cavendish. At first he'd not responded to them, but then ordered them to keep formation.

I detected an air of scepticism amongst my peers, so I found a lonely corner and sat down. Although I knew what had happened up there, the general response I'd received made me doubt myself. Another nip of brandy helped calm the anger and confusion. I looked at the others and wondered if I really belonged amongst them. But I was tired and fragile, it was understandable that some thoughtless action or remark would send me head first into a pit of self-loathing.

We flew twice again that day and it was late afternoon when we touched down for the last time. Shelton watched us taxi in. He appeared excited, like a faithful fishwife waiting for the boat to dock. He was keen to show HB a piece of paper. They had a few words of conversation and then HB called me over.

"Grab your hat lad. We're off for a drive."

"Where to Sir?" I asked.

"Two of your Junkers have been confirmed," Shelton said keenly. "One of them came down about six miles from here. I need to report on the wreckage so we're going over to have a look at it."

By the time I'd grabbed my tunic and cap HB was sitting waiting in the driver's seat of his Alvis Firebird. The canvas hood had been folded down and Shelton sat in the rear with Mabel. The Alvis was much more sophisticated than Mac's Bentley and less garish than Cavendish's MG. The interior was trimmed with a deep red that could have been removed from the state rooms of Buckingham Palace. From the passenger's seat I could see the highly polished two tone black and burgundy paint reflected in the convex chrome of the headlamps. HB slipped the clutch and we headed off with Shelton giving directions from a dog-eared map.

We left the station and turned east. The road verges were thick with vegetation. Every now and then a small intense blob of colour would burst out of the long grass where a wild flower had fought its way through. We passed through picturesque villages with their standard issue stone churches, post offices and bright red telephone boxes.

Shelton patted me on the shoulder with his thin fingers.

"Turns out a Blenheim on its way to Hornchurch was about a quarter of a mile away when you attacked the Junkers. He saw the whole thing unfold and made a report when he landed."

HB smiled at me from the driver's seat and I felt a huge relief. Although neither of them apologised for doubting my story.

The sun had begun to hide behind the taller trees when Shelton pointed up the dusty road.

"That's the spot,' he said after checking the map. We parked on the roadside next to two lorries, painted in that drab green favoured by the army. Mabel was the first out of the car eager to relieve herself against the wheel of the nearest lorry. On the left hand side a short track and wooden five bar gate led to a fallow field.

An infantry soldier was leaning against the gate. His tin helmet was pushed back and a lit cigarette hung loosely between his lips. When he spotted us walking up the track he extinguished the cigarette, adjusted his helmet and picked up his rifle in one swift movement. He brought his arm across his chest and acknowledged the two commissioned officers with a salute. HB replied with a quick flick of the hand to his cap.

"Who's in charge here?" HB enquired.

"The Captain's over there sir." The soldier pointed towards a group of men dressed in khaki.

"What's happened to the crew of the aircraft?"

"They've been taken down to the local nick and an ambulance took the body away about half hour ago, sir." It was then it dawned on me that I'd killed a man.

HB pushed open the gate and the three of us walked through.

The hedgerow had obscured our view, but now I could see the remains of the Junkers I'd shot down. It lay in the middle of the long grass like the carcass of a big game animal. Deep ruts in the ground stretched back showing where the aircraft had skidded across the field before coming to rest. Twisted pieces of the thin metal skin were scattered on the ground where they'd been ripped and torn from the airframe.

The Junkers was facing away from us towards a small copse. The tailfin stuck vertically towards the sky. The dark green paint matched the colour of the oak leaves on the edge of the field. We walked up slowly and around towards the front of the fuselage. There was a slight chill on the evening breeze and a feeling that summer was coming to a close. The port engine had been smashed in the impact and was half buried with its metal propellers bent backwards. I noticed an irregular line of holes which ran over the engine cowling. This was where my gunfire raked across the wing. The cockpit structure had collapsed. The pilot's seat was exposed and the control yoke stood upright and twisted to one side. The rest of the aluminium framework was so badly distorted it was difficult to work out where the crew members sat. There were more of my bullet holes peppered around the cockpit. Beyond the pilot's seat the metal floor pan had survived. Here at the bottom, a pool of blood had collected and congealed. Along the sides the blood had been smeared and I could make out where a stained hand had gripped the side. Mabel who had been rummaging through the brambles appeared at my feet. She surveyed the scene cautiously and then looked up at me with an expression that suggested she knew I was to blame for the blood she could smell.

"What a beauty." HB said as though I presented him with a prize salmon. I smiled awkwardly.

"The bomb disposal boys have already done their bit, so she's safe to poke around in," said Shelton.

I thought about those bombs in the belly of the dead machine. Bombs they'd been carrying to drop on us. I clung to that thought because in my mind I had to justify my actions. It was a machine, a war machine that I destroyed.

While Shelton made out his report, HB requisitioned some tools from the lorries and had some of the soldiers help him cut the black cross from the fuselage. He set to it with an excited physical energy.

"Another souvenir for the squadron." He presented the bent and buckled sheet of metal to me. We covered the rear seat of the Alvis with some old blankets and travelled back to North Weald with my trophy sticking high out of the back seat like the sail of a Chinese junk.

Chapter 18
48 Hour Pass

My fourth week of flying operations. Had it only been a month? It certainly felt a lot longer.

The early morning dew lay heavy on the grass and clung to our boots as we traipsed into the Dispersal Hut. On HB's orders the sheet of metal we'd recovered from my Junkers had been nailed to the wall alongside the other trophies collected from squadron kills. The Adjutant had just finished chalking up the orders for the day on the black board. Freddie nudged my elbow and pointed to the list of names in white letters. Cavendish had been removed from the roster and Aussie was replacing him as the commander of B-flight. The Adjutant noticed our interest and cleared his throat.

"Flight Lieutenant Cavendish has been posted to Central Flying School," he announced and then hesitated as we all stared at him. "They're short of instructors with operational experience. He'll be very valuable to them."

"Poor sods," whispered Freddie. "Imagine him as your first taste of flying in the RAF."

After the first patrol, which was uneventful, both Freddie and I were summoned to the Adjutant's office. He sat behind a wide partner desk which filled the room and barely allowed enough space to pass by either side. The well worn oak surface was partly obscured by piles of beige files and yellow foolscap paper.

A narrow corridor had been left down the centre which allowed for conversation. In the corner of the room sat the clerk, still hammering away on the Imperial typewriter.

"I've got two pieces of good news for you." The Adjutant rocked back on his chair with his hands resting on his pot belly. "The CO has asked me to tell you that you've both been put up for a commission." I was stunned. To gain a commission and become an officer was a burning ambition of mine, but over the month I'd been concentrating on keeping alive and coping with the battle, any thoughts of my own personal development had been long forgotten.

"Now when the paperwork comes through you'll be on a probationary period." The Adjutant continued. "You'll be watched very carefully so behave yourselves!" He leant forward to emphasize the last remark. "Talking of behaving yourselves. You've both been given forty eight hours leave from this evening." He slid two buff coloured chits between the stacks of paper. One had my name on and the other had Freddie's. On both was a large purple stamp with the station name and HB's signature.

"So what are we going to do?" pondered Freddie as we stepped outside. He was holding the pass between his thumb and forefinger as though it was a rare specimen.

"I don't know. Are we supposed to go home?" I suggested.

"I can't do that," protested Freddie. "My parents live in St Ives. I'd spend most of my leave on the ruddy train." He slipped the pass into his inside pocket. "How much money have you got on you?" I detected a plan forming in his mind. I touched my pocket to ensure my wallet was still there.

"About two pounds," I answered.

Freddie squinted in thought and scratched his chin.

"My cousin lives in Westminster. She might put us up, if I can get word to her. That way we could have some fun in town." He looked at me with a mischievous glint in his eye.

I longed to see my family, but I didn't want to go home. I simply couldn't face trying to explain what we'd been through in the last month. I wanted to escape from the battle and not relive it. Besides, who could understand the stress and strain of combat, if you'd not been there yourself.

So it was that we set about making plans for a trip to London. I felt guilty, but justified the decision by assuming that I also didn't have the time to get home and back on duty within forty eight hours. Although I probably did.

Our leave began that afternoon and I was keen to shower and shave before we departed. I was about to head off from the Dispersal Hut when the Adjutant collared me.

"Do me a favour Sommers, the clerk is tied up with the CO, can you drop this off to the Station Commander's office on your way through." He handed me a sealed envelope. This was irritating as it meant a detour on my way to the mess, but I had no choice in the matter.

"Yes sir, right away." I put on my cap and headed off on my errand.

I was walking up the narrow path to Station Headquarters when the door opened in front of me and Cavendish appeared.

I stopped dead and brought my arm up to salute him. He stared at me with his milky grey eyes. He brushed his hair backwards, put on his peaked cap and returned my salute. As he did this I noticed a thin line of recently healed scar tissue which ran across his forehead.

"Well Sommers, I'm off." The corner of his lips quivered in an awkward smile and he strode passed me.

Despite our enquiries we never discovered the reason behind Cavendish's swift departure. Freddie speculated that his behaviour over my Junkers claim may have had something to do with it, but I was reluctant to accept the theory for fear of inflating my ego.

I remembered what Aussie had said about Cavendish having his fair share of trouble and assumed that the scar, hidden by his hair, was the result of a recent painful injury.

The train carriage was warm and filthy, but the seat was well cushioned and comfortable. I stared out of the large window as the fields and hedgerows of Essex hurtled by. We left Epping as the sun was starting to set and purple mare's tails floated high. I had intended to look out for the landmarks I flew over everyday, but very soon the rhythm of the engine rocked me into a deep sleep.

I woke as the train jolted into Liverpool Street Station. Freddie smacked my knee with a folded newspaper.

"Wake up sleeping beauty."

It was dark within the station. Towering above us ornate iron grinders held aloft a canopy of black painted glass. We stepped onto the platform where streams of people moved in every direction. Men in bowler hats fought their way towards the carriages keen, to escape to the suburbs. Men in trench coats ran the other way, hailing taxis. Soldiers, sailors and airmen stood around holding kit bags and smoking cigarettes. A few were kissing goodbyes to pretty girls. Mothers herded their children through the crowds with outstretched arms. One pushed an enormous pram while her faithful husband struggled behind with an oversized suitcase. Everywhere was thick with smoke and grime.

After spending a month between a quiet airfield and the lonely blue sky the sudden mass of humanity made me anxious.

We made for the underground where the air was worse, but the people were fewer. The carriage rattled through the pitch black tunnels deep under the capital until we reached Victoria Station. Here we resurfaced, headed down Vauxhall Bridge Road and cut across Millbank.

Freddie had been successful in wiring his cousin and she had replied saying we were most welcome to stay. She and her husband lived in a modern apartment on Marsham Street. The striking building with its rotund art deco balconies stood high in the street. An aged porter with his brass buttoned uniform eyed us with suspicion when Freddie announced we were calling on Mrs Latham. Reluctantly he criss-crossed the wires on the switchboard and spun the tiny crank handle. He spoke into the mouth piece with an unnaturally deep voice.

"Mrs Latham, I have a …" He looked Freddie up and down. "A Mister Fuller and friend to see you." There was an inaudible reply through the headphones. "Very good." He flicked the switch off.

"She says you can go up." He pointed to the stairs. "Flat three, first floor."

Lucy Latham was a model hostess. The product of a naval family, she'd been born in England, educated in Scotland, finished in Switzerland and had spent many summers in exotic ports wherever the fleet had anchored. She stood in the short corridor waiting for us. Her petite figure was silhouetted by the light that spilled out of the open door behind.

"My dear Freddie!" She had a warm and welcoming tone. Freddie dropped his duffle bag and embraced her in a way only family members do.

"This is Jack." He turned to introduce me. I awkwardly thrust my hand out in a very business like manner. She gently shook it with her soft palm.

"You must call me Lucy." She smiled and I smiled back.

The apartment was large. The hallway opened up into an open plan lounge and dining room. Cream wallpaper with a subtle floral pattern adorned the walls. The furniture was slender and the cushions were thick. The decoration was chic and Lucy in her teal cashmere cardigan fitted the room as though she was modelling the scene for Harper's Bazaar. She showed us our room where she'd made up two narrow beds with blue satin eiderdowns.

"Now I'm sure you boys could do with a drink." I nodded too enthusiastically. "I'm afraid I've not been able to get any sherry, but we do have some scotch."

While she fixed the drinks, Freddie and I sat in two leather lounge chairs. The glass wall-lights cast a warm glow over the wallpaper. London and the rest of the world was sealed out by the heavy blackout curtains. On top of the sideboard was a collection of framed photographs. I recognised Freddie amongst a family group standing on a busy quay at some sailing regatta.

"So Jack, how long have you known Freddie?" Lucy handed me a pleasantly full crystal tumbler.

"About a month, I suppose. I joined the squadron back in July."

"Where do your family live?" she asked.

"Oxford, well just outside."

"Do you know I've never been to Oxford. I must try and get there one day. I'd love to visit the Bodleian." She sat down opposite with a gin and tonic. For half an hour we made small talk about our home towns. She was keen to hear about Freddie's family and news of her other cousins. We sat in a tranquil cosmopolitan atmosphere which was novel to me. For the first time in four weeks I allowed myself to relax.

There was the click of a latch and I heard the front door open.

"That'll be David." said Lucy. "We're in here darling." she called out. I sat upright feeling a little conscious that I was making myself at home in another man's house and drinking his whisky.

"OK, give me a moment." A voice came from the hallway followed by a shuffle and clank.

"You've not brought that darn thing up here again have you?" Lucy questioned. There was no reply. She looked at us.

"It's his bicycle. The last one was stolen from the railings downstairs. He's paranoid about losing this one and insists on bringing it up here."

David entered the room. He was tall and dark and a fair bit older than Lucy.

"Hello Freddie." Freddie and I both stood up as if a school prefect had entered.

"My God the rumours are true! A Fuller in the air

force. Your pop must have had a fit." Freddie's face flushed with embarrassment. David looked towards me and stretched out his hand.

"Hello I'm David."

"Sommers, Jack Sommers." I shook his hand.

Lucy smiled. "Jack and Freddie are on the same squadron up in Essex."

David nodded. "Good show. I bet you boys are being kept busy at the moment."

"Not half," said Freddie. Lucy walked over and David kissed her on her cheek.

"It's beef for supper. I managed to get a rump from Drummond's."

Lucy set off to work in the kitchen while David laid the table. She served the rump with roasted vegetables. It was delicious, but I think the three of us didn't appreciate the effort and time Lucy had spent preparing the meal.

David had opened a bottle of claret.

"It's not the best I'm afraid." He poured out a glass and handed it to me.

"We did have a very good Italian wine man who could source anything you wanted, but David had him deported." Lucy said in an annoyed tone. I looked confused wondering what political powers David wielded.

"Don't taunt me, darling." David finished pouring and stood the bottle in the middle of the table.

"Unfortunately Mr Jenelo was an Italian national and since Mussolini declared war on us all the Italians have been rounded up and sent to internment camps."

"David works at the Foreign Office," Freddie explained and the penny dropped.

"Which had very little to do with the affair," David

179

protested.

"Well no one gave any consideration to our supply of table wines." Lucy teased David.

"I shall bring that up at the next committee." David took a large sip of the wine. To my naive tongue it tasted no different to any other wine I'd experienced. For all I knew I could have been drinking grapes harvested by Dom Pérignon himself.

"Do you think the Italians are a threat?" I found myself asking. David finished his mouthful.

"On their own, no. But with the Germans, yes." He took another sip of the wine and winced.

"We never really worried about the Fascists. I was convinced that the Russians would be a bigger problem." David dabbed his mouth with a white napkin.

"My father always thought the fascists were good for Europe, but he's changed his mind now," I said.

"Yes, a lot of people thought that," David replied wistfully. "I was in the Berlin embassy in 1929. I saw Germany fall on its knees. The door was wide open for the communists to walk in. We knew the KPD, that's to say the German Communist Party, was being controlled by Moscow. They were polling ten to fifteen percent of the vote. Not much less than the Nazis. There was genuine concern about them taking control. The fascists appeared a much better alternative. Of course that was before we really knew what Hitler's ambitions were."

I cut through a slice of beef and pushed it into a blob of horseradish.

"Excuse my ignorance, but what's the difference between a fascist and a communist?" I asked timidly, it seemed a naive question to pitch at a sophisticated dinner table.

"Ha! You tell me," David laughed. "I've met plenty of both far-right politicians and communists activists. There's no difference between the lot although they say they're diametrically opposed to each other." He stabbed a lone potato and waved it in the air. "You can forget the teachings of Marx and Sorel. To be either far right or far left is to be prejudiced, suspicious, anxious and always violent."

"So what's better in your opinion?" Lucy asked. David swilled the remaining cheap claret around the glass.

"Neither. This war is not about policies or ideals. These regimes, communist or fascist, can only work under dictatorship. What we're fighting for is democracy and freedom."

The conversation continued through the beef and on to the desert. I was fascinated by David's stories of where his work in the diplomatic service had taken him. A school trip to Normandy was the extent of my own travels.

After dinner Lucy was keen to put on the radio as a Beethoven recital was being broadcast. We sat in the living room listening to the String Quartet in C Minor and drinking brandy. As the sound of the violin and cello cheerfully bounced up and down I looked at Lucy. The standard lamp cast a shadow across her face and accentuated her profile. I was struck by how beautiful she was.

It was a pleasant evening that took my thoughts far from the battlefield.

Sometime around dawn I woke abruptly expecting to see the duty corporal hovering above my bed. In the pitch black room it took some moments to remember I was not at North Weald. I rolled on to my side, pulled the eiderdown over my shoulder and returned to my comfortable slumber.

At seven thirty I woke again when someone slammed the front door. Freddie lay fast asleep in the bed alongside, unperturbed by the sudden noise. I rose up and pulled back an inch of the heavy black out curtain. A narrow shaft of warm sunlight dissected the room in two. Through the window I looked down on to a square of green grass guarded by a platoon of pollarded plane trees. In the street alongside a milkman playfully swung his basket of empty bottles, while his nag plodded alongside pulling the cart.

I found Lucy clearing the dining table. She was wearing a satin dressing gown with an elaborate print over her silk pyjamas. I was a little embarrassed to find her dressed like this as the gown was low cut, but she was unphased and greeted me with a cheerful smile.

"I hope David didn't wake you when he left." She picked up a cup and saucer.

"No I'm so used to waking early, I struggle to sleep beyond dawn these days." I gently pulled the bedroom door closed behind me. "Freddie's making the most of it though."

"I'm afraid David has to work this morning. I'm becoming a bit of Foreign Office widow at the moment. Do sit down and I'll make a fresh pot," she said disappearing into the kitchen. A moment later she returned with a china rack filled with slices of hot toast.

"Help yourself." She pushed the butter dish and a pot of marmalade towards me. I spread the white butter onto a slice and watched it melt into the tiny dark brown cavities. Lucy bustled back and forth from the kitchen.

"This is marvellous, thank you," I said when she brought through the fresh tea.

"I would have offered you an egg, but I need it for a cake." We were quiet for a moment as I chewed on the toast and she poured out two cups.

"Tell me," she said, pushing one of the cups towards me. "Do you find it frightening flying those planes?" The question caught me midway through a mouthful and forced me to swallow sooner than I'd planned.

"Sometimes, I suppose. I think we've all had moments when we've been scared." It was difficult to compress all the emotions I'd experienced in combat into a few words. She looked at me with her captivating green eyes.

"You know I'm rather jealous. I'm desperate to do something to help the war effort, but David isn't keen on me getting involved."

"What would you want to do?" I asked.

"Well I'm not cut out for the Land Army that's for sure." She chuckled to herself. "Most of my friends are doing something. Two of them joined the Navy last week, but then neither are married and they think it might be a good hunting ground for suitable husbands." She held up her cup with two hands. "I speak French fluently and a little German. I dare say that would be useful somewhere."

"Are there any jobs in the Foreign Office?" I suggested. She chuckled again.

"David would have a heart attack. Can you imagine me working in his department? Mind you I could keep an eye on him there." She was thoughtful for a moment. I looked across the room and over the table. I was struck with a great desire to have a life like this. A well appointed apartment with an attractive and intelligent wife. Yet as I imagined myself in David's position a great fear of commitment and entrapment grew up inside me and wrestled that desire away. I knew it would be some time before I would settle down.

Freddie came through from the bedroom looking dishevelled, but rested. Over a second pot of tea we made our plans for the day.

The three of us spent a relaxing afternoon ambling around Hyde Park. We stopped for a while by the Serpentine and amused ourselves by watching the young men in hired rowing boats attempting to impress their girlfriends with dubious maritime skills. Lucy headed home around five o'clock and we set a course for the West End. I was no stranger to London. As a boy I'd spent many an Easter holiday studying fossils in the Kensington museums and watching the guards change at Buckingham Palace. As a young man, the capital offered adventure in a different way and both Freddie and I were keen to get exploring.

Chapter 19
Nightlife

London is a city that's far too busy to care about who you are and what you do. We sat on the top deck of the packed bus rubbing shoulders with all manner of people. An overweight mother struggled to discipline three children on the backseat. In front two navvies swore viciously at each other in thick Irish accents. A selection of men in suits read newspapers while others in uniforms of various rank and service filled the remaining seats. On public transport all hierarchy and social standing was void, we were all just crammed together waiting for our stop. I felt anonymous and relaxed, a refreshing change from the discipline of squadron life.

We got off by the Theatre Royal and with no particular agenda wandered up towards Piccadilly. At the top of the Haymarket we left the wide road and headed down Jermyn Street where tailors and shoemakers offered temping wares with un-temping prices. Freddie stopped to admire a pair of leather brogues far beyond the range of my weekly wage. An alleyway lined by two stone buildings took us north and we found ourselves in the commotion of Piccadilly Circus. Cars and vans darted quickly between the junctions while open-sided lorries and double decker buses lumbered round the roundabout and the covered statue of Eros. Swarms of people bustled to and fro. Towering above the traffic attached to the smog dirtied buildings were huge advertisements. Bovril and Gordon's Gin were stretched out in ten foot high letters.

An advert for Wrigley's spearmint chewing gum suggested it was good for vim and vigour while another sign told us that Guinness was good for us.

It took some time and an amount of skill to negotiate the vehicles and pedestrians, but eventually we reached Shaftesbury Avenue.

We didn't discuss our route but rather followed a path we had both subconsciously agreed on. We found ourselves in Great Windmill Street staring at the Windmill Mill Theatre. The infamous playhouse where the showgirls stood naked on stage.

"You reckon the rumours are true about that place?" I asked Freddie who was studying the building with great interest.

"Yeah, you know Aussie and Warwick have been inside. Aussie says the girls are completely starkers."

We looked at each other coyly. Freddie shrugged and attempted to speak nonchalantly.

"You want to see if a show's on?"

I felt my mouth dry. I looked around to see if anyone was watching us. I felt nervous, but then again wasn't this the kind of thing that grown men did?

"Ok," I said quietly and we walked up to the narrow entrance. The tall theatre butted awkwardly out into the pavement as though the other buildings were trying to hide it. Maybe they were embarrassed by its presence. Another great sign advertised that the venue was open daily and hosted continuous performances. At street level a glass covered notice board exhibited black and white pictures of the different showgirls a punter might see inside.

Standing in the shadow of the entrance was a burly doorman dressed in a dark overcoat and peaked cap. His nose was kinked and offset. He wasn't a young man but his broad shoulders and stern expression suggested it was not advisable to be on the wrong side of him. We queued up behind a trio of sailors and shuffled towards the ticket kiosk. The doorman said nothing, but looked over each one of us with dark eyes set deep into his heavily contoured face. Under his gaze I felt like a timid school child.

Inside the lights were low and the red flock wallpaper gave off a seedy hue. We entered the auditorium and shuffled through the darkness to two vacant seats. On stage a comedian wearing a tailcoat suit was recounting a story about his mother in law.

"Mind you, I'm not saying she's ugly but when she went on safari a witch doctor used her to ward off evil spirits!" he said in a broad Yorkshire accent. There was a roar of laughter from the audience. The rest of his routine was a series of crude jokes, all of which drew more laughter. I found myself carried away with the atmosphere and joining in.

The comedian finished with a bow and a roar of applause. The stage lights dimmed and the curtain came down. From the orchestra pit came a fanfare and an amplified voice echoed from up high.

"Ladies and Gentlemen, we present to you the world famous girls of the Windmill Theatre."

A testosterone fuelled roar rose up from the crowd. The tinny sound of a tack piano pierced the smoke laden atmosphere and from either wing two lines of scantily clad show girls high kicked their way across the stage. A banjo, tuba and drums joined the piano and the girls opened up with a chorus of 'Roll out the barrel'. While this was happening the curtain lifted to reveal a gauze mesh, behind which three females were silhouetted by a bright white light. On the crescendo of the song the two lines of girls dropped to their knees, the mesh lifted and two spotlights hit the three females. Two of them stood on the lower steps of a small podium, they faced the girl in the middle who stood dead still and completely naked save for a large bonnet which was held in place by a long wide lace chin strap which hung down between her breasts and just covered her lower region. The audience erupted again with shouts and catcalls. At first I found myself too embarrassed to look at the naked form. Instead I looked down towards the orchestra pit, but it was only for a brief moment as boyish curiosity overcame me and I found the courage to study the figure I'd paid good money to ogle. She was a brunette with soft pink skin. Her body was full of curves, from her rounded shoulders into her arched back and round her none too small posterior. Her breasts stood still and upright.

Oddly I found the whole experience far from arousing. I felt more like a medical student at an anatomy lecture than a red blooded male. Anyway we were sitting too far away to make out any interesting details. The show continued with different musical numbers interspersed with an array of more naked women. Although I found it entertaining it was for me less exciting than the anticipation had promised.

An hour and a half passed and the comedian returned on stage to repeat his act. I saw Freddie check his watch and with that we decided to move on.

"I didn't think much of that last one." Freddie was referring to a buxom blonde who'd been posing as the 'Birth of Venus' complete with a large oyster shell.

"Her arms were all podgy and the size of her thighs..!" His biological assessment continued as we stepped out into the warm London evening. When we reached the pavement I felt a firm hand fall on my shoulder. I instinctively ducked and turned half expecting to see a fist heading towards me, but I looked up to find the owner of the hand was Fanshaw the journalist from Epping.

"Now this is a headline. Two respectable Royal Air Force pilots seen leaving a seedy strip club!" He laughed and I felt my face flush with embarrassment. "What are you boys doing in town?"

"Forty eight hour pass," explained Freddie.

"Oh, I see a bit of sight seeing," Fanshaw looked back at the entrance to the theatre. "You boys eaten?" We shook our heads. "Good, follow me." As if leading a platoon of troops into battle, he led us through a network of narrow alleyways and streets. Almost immediately I lost my bearings, but had a notion we were heading west.

It turnout Fanshaw had the use of a friend's townhouse in Mayfair and like us was spending the weekend in town. I asked him why he lived in Epping and worked in London.

"Divorce is expensive and embarrassing old boy," he said as we waited for a road to clear. "Mrs Fanshaw took with her my Kensington apartment, my Lagonda and my collection of first editions when we parted. Fortunately my Aunt moved around the same time which meant I could use her cottage in Epping. I'm not really a country dweller and the trains are a nightmare, but the accommodation is free which is about all I can afford at the moment."

Just before the war Fanshaw had spent two years of his life writing a novel. The four hundred page romantic saga was a financial and critical failure. I assumed his ill-fated literary venture was a major factor in his divorce.

"Here we go, just down here," said Fanshaw as we broke into Berkeley Street from a side road. By now it was getting dark and it was difficult to see the buildings in the blackout. I could just make out the entrances to a few cafes and restaurants. The one we were heading for had a narrow frontage between a second hand bookshop and a cobblers. Above the wide dark door a large sign said François' in decorative Parisian letters.

As we approached, the door opened and a shaft of yellow light spilled out onto the pavement. Another doorman, this time with a slight figure and no broken facial features greeted us.

"Mister Fanshaw, so nice to see you again sir." He greeted us with an earthy, but polite tone.

"Good evening Arthur. These chaps are with me."

Inside, dark mahogany panelling ran down to a cream carpet. A short flight of stairs took us down passed framed art nouveau posters to a set of heavy curtains. The curtains had been hooked back to reveal a basement room crammed full of people. At the far end a low stage protruded towards a wooden dance floor. Around the sides people sat at small tables. Waiters in white jackets darted left and right while two cigarette girls patrolled back and forth. No one was dancing and the stage was bare except for a pianist who was playing a soft and slow composition.

We were ushered to a table near the stage and presented with three menus. On Fanshaw's recommendation both Freddie and I ordered the Coq au Vin Blanc. I was alarmed at the price and estimated I could afford the meal and a single drink before filing for bankruptcy.

"I was sorry to hear about Mac," said Fanshaw as he folded the menu up and gave it back to the waiter.

"We were too," Freddie replied flippantly.

"I hear you boys are doing well up there. How many Jerries have you shot down now?"

"Oh no," snapped Freddie, "We're not talking shop tonight. We're both here to eat, drink, dance and other things if the opportunity arises."

"Alright, if that's the case I'll make sure we enjoy ourselves," smiled Fanshaw.

"But if anyone is asking." Freddie was watching a woman in a silk dress cross the floor. "I've got two kills in my logbook and Sommers has three."

Fanshaw acknowledged the woman and looked back at me.

"You have been busy." He offered around a packet of cigarettes and lit one himself. He exhaled a stream of smoke upwards and thought for a moment.

"I know one of the assistant editors at 'World in Pictures' magazine. I reckon I could persuade him to do a feature on you chaps. I can see the headline now: 'Defenders of the Sky'." He drew his hands across as though he was writing the words in thin air. I laughed at the absurdity of the suggestion.

The meal was served. I was disappointed in its size, but what it lacked in volume was compensated for in taste. Suddenly without explanation Fanshaw stood up and left the table. For a panicked moment I thought he had left the restaurant and we would be stuck with the bill. I was trying to calculate the total we had spent when to my relief he returned. He was accompanied by a man and two women. Fanshaw introduced the man as Evans, an old school friend who was out with his younger sister and cousin. We shuffled our chairs around and Evans introduced the women. His sister Hatty was a tall athletic looking woman with a prominent nose and toothy smile. His cousin Milly was slender with dark hair and a pretty round face.

"So you boys, fighter or bomber pilots?" asked Evans.

"Fighter Command, Hurricanes," I replied quickly with a hint of pride.

"I did a few lessons in a Tiger Moth myself before the war. Over at Hatfield. I was going to join the reserve, but a job came up in the city which was too much money to turn down." There was something instantly dislikeable about Evans. I made the mistake of asking him about his job which gave him licence to speak non stop about his personal and professional experiences. Fortunately, as he was telling us how he had made so much money in American steel Hatty cut him dead.

"Oh do shut up man," she moaned, "so boring." Fanshaw burst out laughing.

"Thank you, Hatty." Evans crossed his arms and glared across the table.

"And just what do you want to talk about?" he grunted.

"Anything but money, politics and this godforsaken war." She turned towards me. "Maybe one of these chaps would like to choose the subject?"

"Don't ask us." Freddie raised his hands. "All we know about is aeroplanes and beer."

"I don't know, aeroplanes and beer sound like a thoroughly exciting way to spend the weekend," said Milly who up till now had been silent. She leant towards Freddy.

"How fast does your aeroplane go?"

"About three hundred miles an hour," he replied.

"Really." Milly's eyes widened. "Have you ever shot another aeroplane down?"

"Never ask a fighter pilot a question like that Milly." Fanshaw interrupted with a wry smile.

Our conversation was halted by the blare of a muted trumpet. I turned to see the pianist had been replaced on stage by a full dance band. The drums, piano and more brass joined in with a toe tapping dance melody. We all sat back and listened. It was a far more sophisticated sound than the tacky tones we'd heard strummed out at the Windmill.

After several stanzas the music softened and the trumpet player stepped forward. As the leader of the band he introduced himself and each of his musicians, then he invited us to enjoy the performance. On cue the music picked up again. Two or three enthusiastic couples emerged from the shadows and headed for the parquet dance floor. I noticed Freddie started to shift in his seat. Acutely aware of his intentions I pushed forward towards Milly and headlong into the attack.

"I wonder if you ladies would care to dance?" I asked Milly. She smiled and took my outstretched hand. Freddie was left with no option but to offer his to Hatty. The four of us stood up.

"You bugger," Freddie whispered in my ear as we moved round. "Why do I get the ugly sister?"

"She's not that bad," I whispered back. "Just don't bang your head on that nose."

When we reached the dance floor Milly stepped in front of me and I gently placed my hands around her waist. I was concerned about intimidating her small delicate frame so left a fair gap between us.

"You'll have to hold me closer than that," she

demanded. Through the delicate silk of her dress I could feel the clasps of her brassiere. Together we launched our feet into a quick step.

As we spun around I noticed the number of people watching us. I became very self-conscious, my legs stiffened and I seemed to lose all form of coordination. Milly stopped and put her hand on my chest.

"Relax, breathe slowly," she said softly. "Feel the music." I did as she instructed and slowly my limbs started to move intime to the music. Gradually my inhibitions ebbed away. At the end of the number she spoke again.

"You're good but you need some lessons."

For the rest of the evening we danced, talked and laughed. All too soon it was over and in the blacked out street we bade each other good night.

I was still thinking about Milly when we headed back to North Weald and the godforsaken war.

Chapter 20
A Change of Tactic

It's remarkable how just a small adjustment can make you feel uncomfortable. On my return to the squadron I was delighted to find my Hurricane was still in one piece, although someone else had obviously been flying it. As much as I tried, I couldn't adjust the seat to a height that suited me. It was the first patrol of the day and the other aircraft were rumbling on to the grass runway. I needed to get a move on, so I raised the seat slightly and pulled out to follow the stream of Hurricanes that were now getting airborne. As the Merlin revved up and I gained speed I felt the seat was still too low. I hesitated on the throttle, wondering if I had time to fiddle with the adjustment again. It was only a brief moment of indecision, but enough to distract me. I let the tail of the aircraft rise far too quickly and with an almighty crack the tips of the propeller clipped the wet ground. The airframe shook and I was thrown forward into my straps. Splinters of wood and tufts of grass flew high into the air. I instantly knocked the throttle back and the tailplane smacked back down. The rest of the squadron thundered past me while I sat in a mud splattered cockpit, fuming at my own incompetence.

Carefully I managed to taxi the aircraft over towards the hangars. Even at a very low speed she shook and quivered like a nervous animal, it doesn't take much to unbalance a propeller.

"You'd better let Edwards know and ask him to bring over another aircraft," said the Adjutant when I reported my mishap. "Fortunately, it's pilots and not aircraft we're short of right now. So, if you decided to have another accident, please don't kill yourself," he added sarcastically.

I found Edwards standing by the fuel bowser with his trusty clipboard in hand. He watched me walking across and read the expression on my face.

"Had a prang laddie?" he asked, knowing full well I had.

"Yes, sorry. I caught the tips on take off."

"That'll be an engine change then," He sighed.

"Is there another aircraft I can take?" I asked gingerly. He flicked over the sheets of foolscap on the clipboard and made a pencil note.

"Yes." he muttered. "We'll bring her round in five minutes."

I thanked him and wandered back to the Dispersal Hut in a despondent mood. Hitting the ground with the propeller would have put a shock load on the engine and could have done a lot of damage. However, this was nothing compared to the enormous dent in my professional pride.

I hadn't been the only pilot to damage an aircraft on the ground that week. Warwick had taxied straight into a temporary machine gun post and Davis had bounced so hard on landing his port undercarriage had collapsed.

As I sat in the crew room feeling sorry for myself the Adjutant came in looking for a spare smoke.

"Did you sort everything with Edwards?" he asked as I offered him a cigarette.

"Yes I don't think he was too happy though."

"Well I wouldn't worry. I've never known a flight sergeant to be happy." He lit the cigarette and sat in the armchair opposite me. "Your commission might come through any day now, so here's a piece of advice. Never overlook the ground crews. They work they're backsides off keeping you guys airborne and safe. I've known too many officers treat the lower ranks badly. If you look after them, they'll look after you. Take a leaf from the COs book. A happy ground crew makes for a good squadron."

It was sage advice. It amazed me how quickly the erks could sweep up a broken aircraft and return it to an airworthy condition, sometimes within hours. As a pilot it was all too easy to take their efforts for granted, and not just the fitters and riggers, an entire army of people worked hard to keep us in the air. They provided us pilots with a comfortable bed, fresh linen, three good meals a day, beer in the evening and a never ending supply of tea and coffee.

I watched Edwards through the filthy window pane and wondered what he really thought of it all. While we dashed around the clouds he fought his battles amongst spanners and screwdrivers, but the war was about to come much closer to home for him.

My replacement Hurricane was a dog. It pulled hard to port on take off and required a generous amount of trim to keep it balanced in the air. I took her up on a mid-morning patrol and when we returned we found a Wing Commander from Group had arrived in an Avro Anson. He was a tubby character with a large bald spot who strutted around waving a piece of paper as though he'd just returned from the Munich peace conference. HB gathered the pilots in the crew room and we sat in two rows of line abreast formation.

"I have an instruction from Air Vice Marshal Park." The Wing Commander barked at us.

"Concerns have been raised over the height that

fighter squadrons are being directed to intercept." He went on to explain that when enemy aircraft were being detected by radar the sector controllers were instructing the squadrons to intercept at an altitude higher than the radar plot suggested. This was to give a height advantage to the fighters. Unaware that any height had already been added to the plot, the squadrons themselves flew higher again for the same reason. This meant that on many occasions the fighters missed the incoming bombers by as much as five thousand feet. This is exactly what had happened to the squadron when I was fortunate enough to score my double kill. We were told that from now on we would attack at the exact altitude given by the radar plots.

Late in the afternoon, after a quiet lunch, the Sector controllers directed us to the most awesome sight I'd ever seen. We had been scrambled and ordered to rendezvous with a squadron of Spitfires from Hornchurch. The Spitfires were more nimble and agile than our Hurricanes and the idea was for us to attack the slower bombers while the Spitfires dealt with their fighter escorts which tended to fly at a higher altitude.

We found the Spitfires waiting patiently for us over Dartford. I heard HB talk to his opposite number and the two Squadrons formed up neatly. I gave a grin to Aussie as he looked over towards me. I couldn't help but feel pretty confident being surrounded by twenty three fighters.

It was one of the Spitfire pilots who spotted the enemy first.

"Bandits two o'clock!" a voice snapped over the radio.

"Bloody hell the skies are full of them!" an anonymous voice replied. To the southeast emerging from the thin cloud was a mass of black dots.

"How are we going to deal with that lot?" Several over voices chipped in, most of them using expletives.

"OK! Keep the chatter down." Came HB's calm and clear voice.

"Panther will take the formation head on," he continued. We wheeled slowly round to face the enemy. Now I could clearly see the shapes of the different aircraft. Over three hundred them spread across the afternoon sky like a biblical swarm of locusts. In that instant I believed all hope was lost. This must be the invasion we had been waiting for. I couldn't see how we could stop such a mighty armada.

"Green and Blue Sections aim for the first wave. Red and Yellow take the second." HB's order snapped me out of my thoughts and reminded me I had a job to do. To hell with it. If this was our last stand we'll go out fighting. With so many enemy aircraft approaching it was strangely difficult to pick one as a target. The waves were made of Heinkel 111s, the heaviest of the Luftwaffe's bombers. Their wide wings and thick cigar shaped fuselages were instantly recognisable. I picked one slightly to the starboard side and began my attack. The damn trim of my Hurricane made it difficult for me to aim. I chewed hard on my lip as I fidgeted back and forth on the controls trying to position the aircraft correctly.

Now within a good range I opened fire, but as I did the Heinkel broke to port and I found myself screaming through the mass of bombers and into the clear air below. I pulled up hard in a loop and rolled off of the top. Now I was above and behind the second wave. I marvelled at the sight of hundreds of aircraft locked in combat. I dived down towards the first target that presented itself. I checked my speed and brought myself in range. The gunners in the surrounding aircraft saw me coming and as I squinted through the gun sight streams of machine gun tracer flew at me from both sides. Thud! Thud! The Hurricane shook, I'd been hit. I kept on chasing that Heinkel, but before I could open fire, another stream of tracers flew past, inches from the canopy. I was in real danger. My instinct took over and I rolled violently to escape. As I did I saw white vapour pouring over my wing and the engine temperature gauge was rising rapidly.

Nevertheless, the bombers had to be stopped. I pushed down again looking for another target. We had been successful breaking up the first formation of bombers, but more were coming. I chased after a lone Heinkel heading north. I jammed the throttle forward, the engine misfired and the jet of steam became thicker. I throttled back and with utter frustration I watched the bomber disappear. My engine temperature was now far too high and it was a matter of minutes before the damn thing would seize. Angrily I pushed the nose down and nursed the stricken aircraft back home.

Once on the ground I leapt from the cockpit and ran round to see what had happened. One of the fitters, Corporal Harris, ran over clutching a pair of wooden chocks. He ducked down under the wings and jammed them in front of the wheels.

"Looks like you got hit," he shouted up.

"I bloody know that." I dived down and joined him. "Where did they get me?" I asked. He pointed to a series of large holes where the machine gun bullets had penetrated. One was very close to where my backside had been resting moments before, another had smashed through the radiator and was obviously the cause of my problems.

"Bugger it!" I thumped the metal cowling. Harris acknowledged my frustration and tried to console me.

"We'll get this patched up alright. Should be back in the air before the end of the day."

I was the first of the squadron to return so I slunk off to the Dispersal Hut and waited. Slowly the aircraft trickled back. Two, however, didn't return. Warwick had suffered a similar fate to me, but had to force land in a field some miles away. He was unscathed but his aircraft was a write off. Davis was the other pilot who didn't return.

Freddie was the last to arrive. He looked strangely frail as he pulled himself out of the cockpit. I hurried over to see what was wrong. He slid down the wing and touched the ground. He turned the metal buckle on his parachute and struggled to free himself from the straps.

"You OK?" I was concerned that he'd been injured. He took a breath and rubbed his hands over his face as if he was trying to remove an invisible mask.

"Davis," he uttered. "His chute didn't open." Freddie looked at me with wide terrified eyes. He lurched forward and vomited. I pulled his parachute straps away and held him up by his Mae West while he composed himself. There's little you can do to help a man who is being sick.

"Thanks," he said softly. "Sorry about that." He looked away from the mess he'd left on the ground.

"What happened?" I asked.

"Didn't stand a chance." A light breeze lifted his matted hair.

"109s. About six of them. They came down as soon

as we got near the Heinkels. I pulled hard and tight and managed to get out, but Davis ended up with two right up the backside. I saw his rudder come clean off. He went straight over on his back." With a shaking hand Freddie produced a packet of crumpled Capstans. We both took one. The smouldering tobacco helped masked the smell of vomit. Freddie continued.

"He came out of the cockpit head first. Nothing happened, he just fell with his arms and legs waving around. I dived down towards him and just for a second I saw his face. His face! The expression on his face." Freddie looked away and took another drag. "You know we were at fourteen thousand feet. He must have fallen for nearly a minute." Watching a man fall to his death is horrific, knowing that while they fall they are alive and conscious, but helpless to their fate.

"I hope to God when I go it's a clean shot to the head," Freddie said.

"All pilots over here at the double!" HB shouted urgently across the airfield. While the aircraft where being refuelled we gathered by the Dispersal Hut and Shelton gave us a briefing. He laid out a map on a trestle table and weighed it down with two mugs.

"It looks like they're throwing everything at us. This might be the invasion." With a broken snooker cue he ran a line on the map from Northern France across the Channel and towards London.

"Early reports suggest Jerry is targeting London. Our concern is this is a decoy to distract from the invasion fleet so keep your eyes open. You need to keep harassing the bomber formations. If you can't shoot the bastards down make sure you knock them off course. Good luck." He withdrew the snooker cue and leant on it as if was a shooting stick.

"As soon as we're all refuelled we're going back up," said HB. "What's our strength?" He looked around and counted our faces.

"Warwick's down in a field somewhere and we've lost Davis," reported Aussie.

"I'm afraid I've got a bullet in the radiator," I said awkwardly. HB looked over at Freddie who was still looking frail.

"Fuller you sit this one out. Sommers take Fuller's kite." It was testament to HB's leadership that he spotted Freddie's fragile condition and used it as an advantage without embarrassing him.

Twenty minutes later we were airborne and flying a wide patrol between Southend and Clacton. By then the raiders had attacked their targets. We held our position until the fuel began to get low and then returned to North Weald. The sun was dipping down behind the horizon. Bright orange rays lay low across the countryside and cast an eerie light on the columns of smoke that grew upwards from the East End. London was on fire. I looked down through the Perspex at the familiar landmarks.

Acres of smoke billowed from the ground and flickering red flames danced here and there. The Docklands, Wapping and Whitechapel were engulfed in a blazing fury, elsewhere smaller fires had broken out. I thought of the places we had visited just a few days ago. I imagined the city in chaos and prayed that Milly, Lucy and all the girls from the Windmill were safe and well.

As the darkness crept over the land my spirits sagged. Surely we couldn't cope with such a hammering. I was convinced the Germans would have invaded by the morning.

Despite our rest in London both Freddie and I had fallen into a bleak state of melancholy. It was a subdued mood in the Kings Arms that evening.

"I reckon we're done for," Freddie moaned, staring at a half full glass of pale ale.

"Don't be so bloody defeatist." Doc clapped him on the shoulder.

"The capital's in flames, we've lost five pilots from this squadron, God knows how many have been lost across the whole of Fighter Command. We're tired and our aircraft are worn out." Freddie pushed Doc's arm away.

"It takes more than a few bombs to destroy a city," said Jakub. We all turned to look at him. It was rare that either of the Czechs engaged in conversation.

"I know from what happened in my country. England is far from fallen. My father always said the darkest hour comes before dawn." His piercing eyes flickered with tenacity. I wished I shared his optimism. The constant strain had drained us emotionally. I was feeling numb and hoping that one way or another the battle would soon be over. I'd lost all perspective on the war. I couldn't see what impact we were or indeed weren't having on the enemy.

I did have one overriding motive that kept me going and that was the loyalty to my squadron and the pilots who flew beside me. Even the toughest of soldiers can't survive for long without his comrades.

Chapter 21
Section Leader

Adlerrangirff was now well behind schedule. Both sides had suffered heavy losses, but the meticulous organisation of Britain's air defences had held the line. The attacks on London marked a significant shift in the Luftwaffe strategy. Goering and some of his staff appeared to be over-confident and convinced that the RAF was close to breaking point. Their intelligence however was flawed and the change of tactic gave Fighter Command a brief respite in which the squadrons could be refreshed and reorganised.

Despite my prediction, the German invasion force did not appear overnight or during the following morning. However, the threat still existed which did nothing to alleviate my anxiety and I started to wish they would try and invade soon, then we would at least know what we were up against.

As always we were stood-to for a first light patrol. Usually all our aircraft were prepared just before dawn, but that morning when we arrived only four Hurricanes were ready.

"What's going on?" I asked Doc who was standing watching the activity.

"Edwards got called away last night. The erks are short handed already and they've been struggling through the night to get the kites sorted."

"Where did Edwards go?"

"His parents' house took a direct hit in the raid yesterday." Doc said quietly. "His mother and sister were killed." Towards the south I could see wisps of smoke in the far distance. Although the enemy had gained practically nothing, our efforts to defend the capital had not been enough. Four hundred and ninety civilians had been killed in London.

The erks were still struggling to position our aircraft. I saw Harris and another man attempting to pull a Hurricane backwards, but the slippery damp grass made the going tough. I jogged over and helped by wedging my back against the tailplane and pushing. The two and a half tons of aircraft moved very slowly. I noticed my fellow pilots who just stood there watching.

"Don't just stand there, give us a bloody hand!" I snapped angrily. It was an audacious reaction. I'd stupidly overstepped the mark by shouting at my superiors, but fatigue had got the better of me. My outburst jolted the huddle of men into action. Aussie sensibly took over the situation and with a combined effort we had all the aircraft ready within a matter of minutes.

Later as we crowded around the stove I apologised to Aussie.

"I'm sorry, I shouldn't have shouted... Sir."

"It's OK, but next time check with me first before you start yelling your head off. It will save a lot of embarrassment." He grinned and walked away.

It was strangely quiet compared to the day before. While we sat waiting for orders, I noticed Warwick's face had turned from his usual ruddy glow to an almost translucent grey. We had all had a few pints the night before and I assumed he was suffering from an overindulgence. However, he kept rubbing his side and rocking back and forth. Then with an almighty cry he doubled up.

"Jesus Christ!" he stammered.

"You OK there?" asked Doc who had also noticed his behaviour. It was apparent that Warwick was ill. Doc gave him a brief examination. He ran his fingers over Warwick's abdomen and prodded gently. Warwick squealed in pain. By now a curious crowd had gathered round including HB and the Adjutant.

"He needs to get to the MO immediately," said Doc without looking up.

As gently as we could we bundled Warwick into the back of a Bedford lorry. Smith the driver crunched through the gears and jerked the vehicle down the bumpy track. It didn't look like it was going to be the most comfortable of journeys.

"What do you reckon Doc?" asked Aussie "Piece of shrapnel in there?"

"Good God no." Doc shook his head. "I'll put a fiver on it that that's just a common or garden appendicitis." Aussie frowned in surprise.

"Even in war time men fall ill." The lorry bounced on a large pot hole and we all winced. "Well maybe Smith will shake his appendix out by the time they get to the MO."

"All pilots on me." HB shouted from the doorway of the crew room and we all ambled over.

"I'm going to change the flying orders." Warwick's malady would now mean reorganising the squadron formations. HB looked at each one of us, scanning our faces with a quick calculating glance.

"Doc, you lead Green Section. Aussie stay as Yellow Section leader and B-flight commander. Sommers." He stopped and looked at me with an expression of deep contemplation. "From now on you lead Red section with Novák and Vaclav as your two and three."

It took a good moment for me to realise the responsibility that had just been placed on my shoulders.

"Yes sir," I acknowledged him with a boyish grin creeping onto my face. Red Section was the rearmost part of the squadron formation and responsible for defending against attack from behind.

With his trademark efficient manner, HB addressed the rest of the squadron.

"Finish your tea and get ready, we're due to be airborne in ten." As the group disbanded he called me over.

"You ready to lead a section?" His curiosity had something paternal in it.

"Yes sir," I replied without hesitation.

"The Czechs work well as a team." He nodded towards Tomáš and Jakub as they walked out to their aircraft. "Use that to your advantage. Don't try and split them up, but do keep them in line." He picked up his flying helmet which was lying limp on the wicker chair alongside.

"Keep your eyes peeled. You're protecting our backside now."

Nine minutes later the squadron took off. I checked over both shoulders and saw the Czech pilots flying neatly behind. Once again we were ordered to link up with a squadron of Spitfires. Together our large formation zigged and zagged over the smouldering sprawl of London, but saw no sign of the enemy. We came back down and spent the afternoon slumped in chairs outside the Dispersal Hut.

These periods of waiting around on the ground were incredibly stressful. I think it was Aussie who coped best with the strain. His philosophy was to live in the moment and take everything as it came. He often said. "If you're sleeping, then sleep. If you're eating then eat and if you're flying then fly, but don't ever worry about what's happening next."

I have a tendency to think too deeply, always pondering about the past and imagining what the future will bring. For me living in the moment has always been difficult. Aussie had lived in the moment most of his life. Happy to travel the world on a whim. As exciting as this sounded he had no roots and little contact with his family, I knew I didn't want to end up like him.

From somewhere a chess set appeared in the crew room. It was fairly old with a battered wooden box and a clothes peg as a substitute for one of the white bishops. I made the mistake of challenging Jakub to a game. I'd fancied myself as a proficient player, Jakub however obliterated my defences and captured my queen with surprising cunning. My king fell into check shortly afterwards and I received a fair bit of stick from the spectators.

As I packed the set away I was surprised to see Edwards standing by the fuel bowser. He was supervising the aircraft movements once again with his clipboard in hand. Barely twenty four hours had passed since his mother and sister had been killed.

On returning to my room that evening I discovered my personal possessions had all been removed. Furiously I marched down the stairs to the duty corporal.

"I'm not bloody dead you know." It was customary for rooms to be cleared quickly after a pilot was killed. "My belongings have all been removed from my room.

Where have they gone?" The corporal raised his dark eyebrows, picked up the desk ledger and then slowly thumbed the pages. He breathed in loudly via his nostrils and looked up.

"All your gear was taken to the Officers' Mess this afternoon," he said in a lazy Midlands accent.

"Why?" I stupidly asked, forgetting about my pending commission.

"Well that's where the officers live. Ain't it," came a flippant reply.

"Very good," I said awkwardly and then walked away quickly.

I was incredibly nervous about life in the Officers' Mess. I'd conjured up an image of something crossed between a crusty old London club and a University College where strict rules and customs were to be followed and obeyed. In fact, it was more rowdy and casual than the Sergeants' Mess I'd been living in up to now.

"You know they'll let anyone in these days." I overheard someone say as I entered the mess for the first time. I turned to see Doc and Aussie sitting by a window and gripping tankards of beer.

"Better get yourself sorted quickly, it's Doc's round next and that only happens every full moon." Aussie raised his tankard.

I was shown to my room by an orderly where I found Freddie was my new room mate.

"You made it over then," He greeted me excitedly. "According to the Adjutant we're on probation, but allowed all the officer perks. He thinks our commissions are likely to come through within the week."

I surveyed the room and took stock. I was

disappointed to leave Jakub behind as he'd become a good friend, but now I was leading a section and within days would be an officer. So much was happening so quickly.

"I'd better write and tell my mother." As I went to close the door behind me I noticed a small brass frame which held a piece of card and the names of the officers who occupied the room. This one hadn't yet been changed and in unevenly typed letters it read Flying Officer P Davis. I stared at it, aware that Freddie was watching me.

"You know every time I close my eyes to sleep I see him falling."

Chapter 22
One on One

It was a huge relief to find that the heavens had opened and rain was pouring down the next morning. B-flight was stood-down until lunchtime and I seized the opportunity to sleep off another horrendous hangover. Aussie and Doc had decided to initiate me and Freddie into the mess with a large amount of alcohol. I can't say I was one hundred percent recovered by the time we gathered in the crew room, but the extra sleep had been a godsend.

The telephone rang and the corporal picked up the receiver. Each of us stopped what we were doing and watched him as he scribbled on a notepad. He turned to HB who was sitting beside me.

"Lone bandit. Angels fifteen over Clacton. Scramble one aircraft."

HB punched my arm.

"Go on then Sommers, your turn."

. . .

"Panther three airborne over North Weald." I was at a thousand feet and speaking to the sector controller a matter of moments later.

"Okay Panther three, vector zero eight zero make angels sixteen." Came Aunty's throaty reply. The weather was foul, thick grey clouds hung barely three hundred feet over the airfield.

I rose up into the ominous sky and in a moment was enveloped by the cloud. Deprived of any visual reference I was instantly disoriented and glued my eyes onto the instruments in front of me to ensure I didn't stall, spin or invert myself. The Hurricane pushed on with the great Merlin engine pulling me up through the vapour. There seemed to be no end to the cloud. I climbed higher and higher, still I was engulfed by white nothingness and I started to wonder if I was climbing at all. Suddenly at two thousand feet the cloud thinned and I burst into brilliant sunshine. The sun rays penetrated the Perspex and warmed my cheeks. Below in every direction was now an ocean of white and above was a deep blue atmosphere. It was as if I'd been transported to another world. I was climbing still and the plateau of cloud fell away beneath me. With no landmarks to see I called the sector controller for a fix.

"Vector zero seven zero now, you are heading too far south." Was Aunty's curt response. Three or four minutes passed and the radio crackled again.

"Panther three, bandit now three miles east of you. Angels one four." I strained my eyes. In this crystal clear atmosphere I should be able to see the aircraft at three miles. I continued to head eastwards. The chances were this was a lone Jerry, most probably taking advantage of the cloud for a quick photo reconnaissance.

"Catnap, this is Panther three. No bandit's insight." Surely they'd be visible by now?

"Panther three, continue to search the sector."

I flew a pattern of wide circles looking above, below and everywhere. The radio crackled again.

"Panther three, we've lost the radar plot. Call it off and head home."

For good measure I flew one last circle and mused over how efficient these radar plots were. They appeared to be good at spotting large raids, but single aircraft were a different matter.

Well below me I could see the edge of the weather front. The expanse of cloud came to an abrupt end and I could now see the glittering North Sea. Free from the constraint of formation flying I decided to do a bit of sightseeing. In a gentle dive I headed towards the clouds' margin. The sight was amazing and well worth the journey. The bank of pure white cloud stood a thousand feet tall. It was like a large everchanging cliff face. I swooped down and then up, like a child on a swing. I flew alongside this strange white landscape allowing my wingtip to touch the edge of the vapour. With the stress and strain of the battle I had forgotten the freedom of flying and in that moment rekindled those emotions I'd felt on my first solo flight.

Inevitably it wasn't long before my thoughts were drawn back to my duty. I levelled off and rose up once more above the clouds. Just before I set course for home I allowed myself one last glance at this amazing vista. It was lucky I did so as when I turned I saw an aircraft about a thousand feet above me and diving towards my tail. It was a Messerschmitt 109. He had the perfect angle on me and was closing rapidly. In three or four seconds he would open fire. My first instinct was to push down away from him, but I was now a veteran of many dogfights and knew he would expect me to do just that. Instead I went against the textbook teachings.

I throttled back and waited until I judged I was in range of his weapons, then I pulled the nose up hard. I lost a lot of forward speed very quickly, as a result he overshot and flashed over the top of my canopy. We passed close enough for my Hurricane to shake and buffet in his wake. I rolled straight onto my back and dived down.

Now I regained the speed I'd lost. I briefly levelled off and pulled hard to starboard. The 109 had recovered and was turning towards me. We were on two converging paths which would bring us head on to each other. This had now become a deadly duel. If either of us were to break away we'd give the other the advantage and a clean shot. I was chewing my lip, the safety ring was set to fire. Incensed by his attempt to attack me unaware, I resolved to finish my opponent by either bullets or collision. The two aircraft closed rapidly towards each other. In flying straight towards him, I found it difficult to judge his range. I took no chance and pressed the gun button. All eight of my Brownings opened up. I saw a brief flash from his wings. I kept firing until we were only feet away from each other. There was an almighty crack and the Hurricane juddered. I could see nothing, I'd lost my vision. I thought he hit me, but there was no pain. I blinked hard, hold on, I could still see everything inside the cockpit. My vision was clear but dead in front of my eyes the inch thick plate of bullet proof glass had cracked and shattered.

How on earth we didn't collide with each other I don't know. I believe his nerve gave in at the last moment and he pulled up. I turned hard again, ready to face him once more, but he was flying away from me with a thin line of black smoke trailing behind. This gave me time to assess my own damage. I had not been injured, the engine was running fine and the aircraft was handling well. My only concern was I had no forward vision, it would be impossible to aim at another aircraft. Through the side panels I could now see the 109 losing height. I was concerned he might attempt to cross the channel and live to fight another day. I had to finish him off. I gained on him quickly and brought my aircraft behind his, although I was unable to see if he was in my sights. I then understood why he was losing height and it had been easy for me to gain on him, his engine had seized. The black three bladed propeller had stopped dead. Along with the heavy Daimler Benz engine it had become a dead weight which was pulling him earthwards. He didn't stand a cat in hell's chance of crossing the channel. I twisted the gun button to safe and very gently pulled alongside the stricken machine. I was curious to see what I'd been shooting at. The small 109 was a pretty machine. The light grey fuselage was stained with black streaks. I slipped alongside with caution as one might handle a drowsy wasp, just in case it had some sting left in it. The canopy had been jettison and I could clearly see the pilot. He looked over towards me. His helmet and oxygen mask obscured his features but even at that distance I thought I could see a mournful expression in his eyes. I raised my hand with an open palm in a pathetic gesture of peace. He nodded in response and then bowed his head back into the cockpit and towards the expanse of sea. The exchange of expression which lasted a matter of seconds felt like a ridiculous end to a chivalrous duel. He had attempted to kill me, I had attempted to kill him.

Oh what I'd have given to rescue him from that doomed aircraft. To have spoken to him, to have found out what these men were really like. Were they villainous, murderous beings or were they just like us, but with black crosses painted on the wings instead of the red white and blue?

There and then I could have easily landed, switched

off my engine and walked away from war and conflict had it not been for my overriding sense of duty and something I'd just spotted. Forward of the Messerschmitt's cockpit, on the engine cowling was a symbol. A red circle within which was the character of a devil firing a bow and arrow. I'd seen that symbol before, on the machine that killed Mac. It was impossible to tell if this was the same aircraft or even the same pilot, but it was definitely the same unit. An eye for eye? If I had just avenged Mac's death it didn't give me the satisfaction I'd imagined it would have done.

At a thousand feet I waggled my wings in a sign of friendship and pulled around to the west hoping the German would follow. He seemed reluctant to jump and his best option now was to ditch as close as possible to the shore. He ignored my gesture and carried straight on out to sea.

From a distance I watched him glide down and gently touch the green waves, which appeared to calm as he touched the water. Before I could get overhead the little aircraft had sunk and no sign of life emerged. The waves rose again as if to say he's mine now.

Back at North Weald my aircraft was given a full inspection, but the only damage found was that single seven point nine two millimetre machine gun bullet embedded in the glass. It was a perfect shot for if the glass had failed it would have taken my head clean off. The glass and bullet were removed, mounted on a wooden plaque and hung on the crew room wall as another trophy of our war.

Chapter 23
Sleep

I lay in a dead sleep oblivious to the world outside my slumber. A low moaning sound emanated from somewhere. It passed, but then returned a moment later, this time louder. Then it became a shout. I opened my eyes. The room was pitch black, but I could just make out where the sound was coming from. It was Freddie twisting and turning in his own bed, fast asleep but reliving the tragic moment of Davis' death.

"Freddie," I whispered in an attempt to stir him from his nightmare. I went to his side and shook his shoulder. "Freddie," I said louder. He opened his eyes and stared at me. His hand gripped my wrist, I couldn't tell if he was awake.

"Freddie, it's okay," I said calmly. Comforted by my presence his grip weakened to a gentle squeeze. His eyes slowly shut and his body rested once more.

Chapter 24
The Interview

"Can we have two of you sitting on the wing. The rest of you gather here. That's right. Squadron Leader in the middle." The photographer in his Burberry mackintosh and fedora hat manhandled us into position with urgency. He had been sent along to accompany Fanshaw who had carried out his threat and managed to sell our story to World in Pictures Magazine.

Freddie and Jakub climbed up on the wing of a Hurricane while the rest of us gathered around HB. Set at our feet were three of our war trophies. The black cross that HB had salvaged from my Junkers, a yellow propeller spinner from a 109 brought down by Aussie along with a German machine gun, the barrel of which was bent at ninety degrees. Mabel stood faithfully at HB's side. Although we were off duty the photographer had asked us to pose with our flying gear on. I wore my Mae West over my shirt sleeves and held my helmet in my hands. My Mae West was filthy, sweat, oil and tea stained the front. We all looked fairly unkempt, but were told the magazine wanted realism and were forbidden to groom ourselves.

"OK gents, everyone looking at the camera."

There was a click and the photographer pushed and pulled the plate from the back of his Speed Graphic camera.

"Now can we have some individual pictures." There was a united groan from the group. We all felt very awkward. The photographer turned to Fanshaw for some direction.

"Yes we need the CO and Sergeant Sommers."
Fanshaw pointed and winked at me. I found myself at
the mercy of my comrades and was attacked with a
variety of friendly insults and cat calls. Why on earth
had I been singled out? I wasn't happy with the whole
affair. It was ridiculous that in the middle of a vicious
battle we were posing for photographs.

The group disbanded and I was positioned in front
of the Hurricane propeller.

"Do try and relax, it looks like you just sat on a hot
poker," said Fanshaw over the shoulder of the
photographer.

"Try looking up to the sky, as though you're
longing to get back in the air." I looked up but all I
could do was squint. I felt my face turning crimson,
thank God these were black and white photographs.

"That's better, hold it there." Click went the camera
again and my image was committed to film.

. . .

"Just to check some details. You were born in
Oxfordshire? Did you always want to be a pilot?"
Fanshaw fired a volley of questions at me.

"Err, I suppose I was interested in flying as a
child."

"And you joined up last year?"

"Yes."

"Are you proud to be flying in the RAF?"

"Well, yes. I mean who wouldn't be."

"What do your family think about you being a
fighter pilot?"

"Um, not sure. I think they're happy." I was
enjoying Fanshaw's interview far less than posing for
the photographs. We sat opposite each other in the

crew room with the journalist scribbling illegible notes in a pocket book. The duty corporal sat at his desk and I was conscious he could hear everything I was saying.

"What do you think of the war?" Fanshaw continued. "Do you reckon we'll win?" He looked up from the notepad.

"You're asking the wrong person. We have no way of gauging ours or Jerry's strategy. Sometimes we go up and the sky is crawling with swastikas and other times it's completely empty." Fanshaw rested his fountain pen.

"What's your biggest fear? Are you frightened of death?"

"Death? No, I don't fear death. I saw it the first day I arrived here. Since then in one way or another it's stayed with me everyday. What I fear is failing at our duty. Coming home to find my family or friends have been killed because I didn't do my job and let the bastard bombers through. Or losing a pilot because I wasn't quick enough to react to the Messerschmitt on his tail. That's my biggest fear."

Fanshaw sat back in the armchair. He screwed the lid back on his pen and slipped it into his inside pocket. He studied me closely and then closed his notepad.

"What's it like up there?" From his coat pocket he took a packet and offered me a cigarette with exotic French writing down the side.

"It's a magnificent world up there." I took a cigarette and he lit it with a silver lighter that looked familiar.

"The sky is never the same. The clouds are constantly changing and the colours are much more vivid than any artist can paint, but we spend our time flying forwards and backwards in rotating patterns searching and searching for the enemy. When he appears, it's over in seconds and you've nothing to do but head home and refuel. That's if you're lucky enough to still be in one piece." I sucked on the cigarette and let the smoke stream from my nose. "Up there it's exhausting."

I didn't know why Fanshaw had singled me out to interview, other pilots had far more interesting stories to tell and I was still comparatively junior to most of them. I wasn't keen for any publicity, but that interview had a great effect on me. For the first time I'd spoken to a person outside of the squadron about what we were going through. It was a cathartic experience to describe my feelings and say them out loud. Afterwards I felt I had a better sense of proportion on the battle.

Unfortunately for Freddie he was losing his perspective on the situation. His checky sparkle that got him in and out of trouble had disappeared. He had become increasingly inward facing and looked physically weaker. He was the same age as me and although he came from a wealthier background and had joined the squadron a few weeks before me, we were peers. It was impossible to think about him without drawing a parallel to my own life. Now as I found the strain of war was thickening my skin I could see Freddie starting to become more and more fragile. Almost every night he woke up, crying out in a cold sweat.

About this time we were joined by more pilots. Paul Muller was a Lieutenant seconded to us from the Royal Navy. With his Germanic surname he had been given the nickname of Fritz. Although he swore blind that he was fifth generation English. He was an experienced pilot who had been flying Gloster Gladiator Biplanes off HMS Courageous.

Three younger pilots had also been posted to us. One pilot officer and two sergeant pilots. They arrived one morning while we were in the air and we found them huddling together in the crew room looking nervous. Remembering how daunting those first days on the squadron were for me, I felt compelled to speak to them and put them at ease. I approached them holding a mug of tea and the standard packet of Craven A to offer, but before I got halfway across the room HB cut me up with a purposeful stride.

"What hours on Hurricanes?" he asked curtly. The three newcomers jumped to their feet. The young pilot officer spoke first.

"Four hours, sir." Then the sergeants spoke.

"Five sir." and

"Four hours sir." HB's shoulders drooped and he let out a sigh.

"Okay don't get comfortable." He shot out of the room calling for the Adjutant. I abandoned my welcoming party and withdrew outside where Aussie was sitting. Through the open window we overheard a series of heated telephone calls and then HB emerged from his office swearing.

"Ruddy ridiculous, sending us kids with just a few hours on type. We haven't got time to mollycoddle them. We need experienced pilots for God's sake." Aussie nodded, I said nothing. When I'd arrived I didn't have many more hours, but then the battle wasn't as intense as it was now.

"What's happening to them?" Aussie asked.

"I've told the Adj to send them back to Group. The

Wingco won't like it, but I couldn't care less." It was shocking to see such an outburst from HB, like the rest of us he was starting to show signs of fatigue and his temper was fraying. Surely it couldn't be long before some higher authority pulled us out of the front line for respite.

Chapter 25
The Lark Ascending

We had returned from yet another dawn patrol and seen no sign of the enemy. A thin band of September mist stretched over the county and the damp air penetrated our cockpits. To the east the warmth of the low sun was diluted by the overcast sky. To the south more wisps of white smoke curled upwards where a flickering orange glow had hung there in the dark. London had been attacked again last night.

I had an ominous feeling from the moment I arrived on the airfield that morning, like the heavy pressure you feel before a thunderstorm. We gathered outside the crew room while Edwards and his team of mechanics, fitters and armourers prepared our aircraft once again.

We looked a peculiar lot. We were all young, but our faces belonged to older men. Each set of weary eyes had their own story to tell, every pair strained and scarred by weeks of flying and fighting. Freddie sat alongside me, continually rubbing his hands and fidgeting with his fingers.

Ever so slowly the clouds dispersed and the morning dew evaporated in the warm sun. A newspaper lay discarded on the table beside me. I considered picking it up, but then thought against it. I knew all I wanted to know about this war and was fed up with the speculation and opinion of others. Everyone was quiet and still like pious monks in deep contemplation. I wiped a mud stain from the sleeve of my flying jacket and flexed my elbow. The jacket felt more comfortable but was still a little stiff around the shoulders.

There was a click as Jakub undid the catch on his violin case. Aussie rolled his eyes disdainfully. Fortunately, Jakub was none the wiser. He took out the instrument and wiped down the veneer with a four by two square of cloth. Holding it in his left hand he tucked the rest under his chin and with his right hand he plucked playfully at the strings.

Three Hurricanes from another squadron roared past us, putting up a flock of rooks in the process. As the aircraft disappeared and the rooks eventually calmed down, a gentle bird song drifted across the airfield. Jakub looked over towards the sound. He cocked his head slightly and listened.

"Ah the lark?" he asked excitedly. I turned my head, but having no idea what a lark looked or sounded like, I simply shrugged my shoulders.

"It is the lark." He affirmed and then picked up his bow. Ever so gently he began to play.

With his fingers dancing on the fingerboard he drew the bow over the strings. His whole body began to move and from deep within the violin came Vaughn Williams' tranquil melody that perfectly mimicked the lark's song. Everyone was silent as the notes resonated from the instrument. As I listened, I found myself slowly drifting into a serene state of meditation. The movement transported me from that mud splattered, battle scarred airfield and into thoughts of wide open spaces, lush fertile scenery and an overwhelming sense of freedom.

Like a vicious blow from a sledge hammer the telephone shattered my meditation.

"Large hostile formation! Squadron scramble!" The corporal shouted. We were on our feet and running to our aircraft. Edwards already had my engine running as I slung the parachute over my shoulders and buckled the all important crotch strap up between my legs. I clambered up into the cockpit with swift movements and an energy that only adrenaline can produce. The wash of the prop was hard on my face until I slid down behind the windscreen. I plugged in my headset and oxygen. Edwards grabbed my shoulder. I looked up.

"Give 'em ruddy hell!" He shouted over the noise of the engine. He had a fierce glint in his eyes. I smiled at him and pulled down my goggles.

Everything in the cockpit looked good, oil pressure, engine temperature, fuel. Look to port - Jakub's engine was starting. Look to starboard - Tomáš was already running. Wait a few seconds for Jakub. A wave of my hand to Edwards, who was now on the ground, and the wooden chocks were tugged away. Ease the throttle forward and I was taking off. I left the ground with my section as I'd done countless times during the last two months, but this time a strange icy feeling seemed to grip my heart and although the instruments said everything was right I felt something was out of place, as though I'd forgotten something.

"Panther this is Catnap, I have some trade for you. Vector, zero four seven. Angels one eight," came the familiar throaty voice from down below.

"Roger Catnap. Panther vector zero Four seven and climbing," HB responded. At ten thousand feet we rendezvoused with a squadron of spitfires and headed South East.

"Panther leader, four bandits on our two o'clock about a thousand below," came a sudden and urgent voice, I think it was Doc. Sure enough heading to the west maybe a mile away was a group of aircraft. At that distance it was impossible to identify them, but from the way they were positioned and the direction they were travelling suggested they were hostile. The radio crackled again as another pilot confirmed he'd spotted them too. HB cut across the airwaves.

"Panther leader to Red One, take Red Section over to investigate." As this wasn't the large hostile force we'd been sent to intercept, HB ordered only my section of three aircraft to chase them down.

"Roger, Panther Leader," I acknowledged HB's order and then waggled my wings to inform Tomáš and Jakub we were going to turn. "Red Section turning west," I told them.

I felt my limbs stiffen as I turned the aircraft. For a few brief minutes I'd started to relax, enjoying the mid morning vista and letting my thoughts wander from the task in hand. The four black dots now in front of me brought me back to the present dangers. As the adrenaline started to flow again a pain shot through my stomach. It was quite a different feeling from the nausea and tension I often felt before getting airborne, this was sharper, more acute.

With our noses slightly down, the three of us raced towards the targets. I calmed myself with a lung full of oxygen and checked around the cockpit. Engine still looked fine, the reflector gunsight was on.

The black dots were getting bigger, but what were they? The wings were too thin to be the large Heinkel bombers, they could be Ju 88's, but hold on were they British? Could they have been a flight of Blenhiems returning from a sortie over the Channel? No wait. The nearest aircraft banked slightly showing the distinctive profile of a German Dornier Do 17 bomber.

I selected one on the starboard side as my target and throttled back slightly.

"Tally Ho Red Section!" I called frantically over the radio. The Dornier was still flying straight and level and converging onto my aim. A sudden flash of brown and green caught my eye as Tomáš' Hurricane sped past me.

"Bloody idiot, he'll overshoot," I said to myself. The Dornier was still there in front of me, becoming closer and closer. Wait, wait until it's well within range. 600 feet now, too far to shoot but tempting, 500, 400. Then before I could fire the Dornier broke sharply to the right. I pushed the stick over and followed. Just for a brief second the long fuselage passed through my gunsight. I pressed the gun button and fired, but my reaction was too slow and he was out of my aim before I could do any damage.

I berated myself. "Calm down man, think straight!"

The Dornier pitched down to pick up speed and then broke left. I anticipated the move and this time my aim was better. Once again my machine guns fired.

I could see the pilot in the cockpit of the Dornier as I hit his starboard wing with a volley. I weaved dramatically, preventing the rear machine gun from getting a bead on me. The Dornier pulled tighter into the turn and then banked sharp right. The force of the manoeuvre smashed the gunner against the canopy. I managed to stay with it but I still could not get a clean shot. In the matter of seconds that had passed our two aircraft had descended by five thousand feet.

The Dornier held the turn and we continued to spiral down. In an effort to break the deadlock I banked and briefly dipped below the German. With the extra momentum I'd gained, I pulled back and rose quickly up underneath the him, I fired again this time holding the button for longer. The sky blue paint of the German wing filled my gunsight as we passed within a matter of feet. Now I was higher and had to roll out of the climb. Some distance was now between us, but over my shoulder I could see a stream of white smoke coming from the starboard engine of the Dornier.

The only thing that would save the German now was speed. He divided again and I was back on his tail and within range. I fired a short burst, which hit the other engine, surely he was going down. I flew straight and level waiting to see what would happen. There was an almighty bang in the cockpit, glass and metal ricocheted around my head. Some hard invisible force pushed my hand from the throttle and a searing pain pieced my chest. In my excitement I'd forgotten about the rear facing machine gun. Flying level for just a few seconds had given the gunner a chance to fire back. The Dornier banked to the left and away from the Hurricane.

I tried to compose myself. I was angry, frustrated and bleeding. Below I could see the Dornier racing away, now leaving a thicker trail of smoke behind. I dived once more to catch him. We were at six thousand feet, and he needed more speed to outrun me. The pain in my chest had become more intense. I tore the mask from my face, we were now well below the need for oxygen. Three thousand feet and the Dornier started pulling out of the dive. Two thousand feet. I scored a few hits on the side of the fuselage with another volley of bullets, but I overshot and had to turn hard for another attack. The Dornier was running out of height, I wanted to force him to climb then his aircraft would slow and become an easy target.

A thousand feet now. I had him back in my gun sight, surely I'll finish him this time. Below the Sussex countryside with its freshly harvested fields flashed past. A steam train charged across the country towards the town of Redhill. Five hundred feet now.

Sweat poured from under my helmet and ran into my eyes. My gloved thumb found the gun button and firmly pushed it in. The Brownings rattled and then stopped. I looked down, my thumb was still on the button, I pushed again, nothing happened.

We were so low now my altimeter couldn't register the height. I looked over both of the wings and tried to fire once more, nothing happened. In my determination to shoot down the Dornier I had spent all of my bullets. I was now angry, frustrated, bleeding and out of ammunition. But I refused to quit, if I stayed on the Dornier I might force him into a mistake or be able to draw another aircraft into the fight.

The pilot of the Dornier, having no idea of my predicament, continued to fly low over the countryside. Remarkably his engine had still not seized and was able to keep the speed up. We thundered over a church steeple rattling the windows in a sleepy village. A cart horse startled by the roar of our engines reared up. I was still pinned on the Dornier's tail but managing to keep myself slightly above and out of the gunner's aim. We passed over farmhouses, fields, cattle and sheep. Over hedgerows, woods and rivers. I saw a butcher's boy cycling on a narrow lane throw himself headlong into a ditch.

For twenty miles I pursued the Dornier at low level. The coast was now in sight. I was incandescent with rage and determined not to allow this unwelcome intruder to escape. I believe the pilot of the Dornier now realised I was out of ammunition and no longer a threat, because he started to climb.

He had made it to about eight hundred feet when my emotions got the better of me. In desperation I swept around towards the Dornier, as if I was going to attack it, then dropped below my opponent and quickly flicked my port wing upwards. I'd hoped to clip his rudder, but instead the tip of my wing smashed into the narrow fuselage of the Dornier at a right angle. The collision severed the metal like a clumsy woodman's axe. The wide tailplane was separated from the rest of the aircraft. With no lateral stability the grey green aircraft lost its ability to fly. It plummeted nose first towards the earth.

The impact shook my Hurricane violently and I smashed my head against the side panels of the canopy. I had no time to assess the damage that I'd done to my adversary as the collision had also ripped off the tip of my own wing. My momentum had carried me upwards but as I levelled off I saw the aileron on my port wing tear away from its fixing. Now I was without control of my wings. I knew there was no chance of landing successfully, I had to abandon the aircraft.

I pulled the canopy release and slid it back firmly. With the fingers of my left hand I yanked the pin release buckle on the harness which freed me from the seat. I paused for the briefest of moments wondering if this was the right thing to do, but I could see no other option. I let go of the control column, quickly put both hands on the cockpit sides and stood up. The slip stream over the fuselage pushed me back and pinned me to the bulkhead behind. With no hand on the controls the aircraft pitched violently downwards which shot me out of the cockpit. There was an almighty thump on my left elbow as the rudder smashed into me and sent me spinning in the air. I was completely disoriented, unsure if I was upside down or travelling vertically. I fumbled furiously and managed to grab the metal ring on my left hip. With every ounce of strength I could muster I pulled the ring. The connecting wires parted the canvas flaps of the parachute pack and a fountain of white silk shot skywards behind me. The canopy of the parachute billowed out above and with a painful jolt, my fall was arrested. The canvas straps bit into my inner thighs and I exhaled sharply as the sudden deceleration shot the air out of my lungs.

After the tremendous tumult of the last five minutes everything was quiet and strangely peaceful. Dangling hundreds of feet above the earth I tried to make sense of what had just happened.

As the adrenaline diluted and the feeling of shock subsided, I became acutely aware of my injuries. My hand throbbed, blood was oozing from my chest and my elbow had gone numb. I was heading rapidly towards the earth when suddenly a gust of wind rose up and steadied my decent. Despite this I still hit the ground with a violent impact. Without the weight of my body the dome of white silk above sagged and floated down. The text books will tell you to release your parachute as soon as you land to prevent the wind dragging you along the ground, but my elbow was so painful I couldn't bend my arm to undo the buckle of the harness.

I lay on the earth staring up at where I'd just fallen from and giving thanks for reaching terra firma in one piece. I tried to sit upright, but as I pushed myself up from the ground the pain in my arm was unbearable. I assume at this point I fell unconscious. My memory has no narrative except for snatches of conversation which were spoken above me. I vaguely remember two dark figures and someone saying

"I've got a pulse." and another person talking about "Southlands not far." I came round briefly and felt I was moving in a vehicle although I didn't open my eyes. Then there was a very bright white light and more shadowy figures moving above me.

. . .

I became aware I was lying in a bed. I felt my body was restricted, but I was comfortable. Gingerly I attempted to open my eyes unsure of what I would see. Everything was dark and I blinked to check I had actually opened my eyes. I could make out the fuzzy outline of a cast iron radiator, then a desk and a lamp. I shifted my body so I could see more of the unfamiliar landscape, but found that my left arm was completely restricted. I groaned trying to make sense of what was going on. Something moved swiftly in the darkness.

"It's okay," came a soft female voice. "You're safe."

I relaxed my shoulders and tried to see where the voice was coming from.

"Where am I?" I stuttered.

"You're in hospital, but you're alright." In the shadows alongside my bed I could now make out a pretty smiling face.

"Rest, you must rest." the voice said again and I felt two dainty hands gently roll my shoulders back onto the pillows. I gave up any thoughts of resistance and drifted back into darkness.

Chapter 26
Rest and Recuperation

Over the following days I managed to deduce what had happened to me. My fight with the Dornier and subsequent collision had been witnessed by a fair few people as the final stage took place over a small village. After the collision the Dornier crashed on the outskirts of Shoreham, there were no survivors. I bailed out at nine hundred feet which gave little time for my parachute to open, but fortunately I fell into a field of stubble and the warm air rising from the bald earth beneath me helped to slow my fall.

A local doctor had been on his rounds attending to a pregnant woman when he saw me coming down. He was one of the first on the scene and seeing I was in a fair amount of pain, administered a large shot of morphine which accounted for why I couldn't remember much. The little finger on my left hand was badly lacerated and I had a puncture wound in my chest. It's impossible to tell exactly what happened but it is reasonable to assume a bullet entered the cockpit through the airframe, hit the throttle quadrant cutting my little finger and then ricocheted up into my pectoral muscle. By the time it hit my chest it would have lost a fair amount of momentum and only had enough force to rip through my uniform and lodge itself just below the skin. It still hurt like buggery though. My left arm then hit the rudder when I jumped from the cockpit. The impact fractured my elbow and was excruciatingly painful.

I was taken to a local hospital where the medical staff were able to remove the bullet from under my skin, patch up my little finger and reset my elbow. I spent four days in that hospital and remember very little, but the image of that sweet female face in the darkened room stayed with me for years to come.

With my wounds still healing I was dispatched via train to Weston-super-Mare. Here a hotel had been requisitioned for recuperating officers. (While I was dangling in my parachute my commission had come through.) The mixture of stodgy food, sea air and boredom ensured I made a speedy recovery.

The day of my incident was a turning point in the war. The Luftwaffe had sent huge numbers of bombers against us and they had suffered very heavy losses. German High Command now realised they had failed to smash the Royal Air Force. The official record states that the Battle of Britain lasted until October 1940. For me though, it ended on the fifteenth of September.

My days at Weston-super-Mare mainly consisted of walking up and down the promenade and playing cards with the other casualties. One afternoon while I was staring out of the large sash window watching a tramp steamer chugging up the Bristol Channel, I heard a commotion from the hotel lobby. Three familiar faces appeared at the lounge doorway. Doc Delaney, Aussie Packard and Warwick had fought their way past the reception desk.

"Tally Ho, bandits at six o'clock!" shouted Aussie.

"We thought we lost you for good," said Doc.

I stood up to greet them. Aussie whistled a high pitch note.

"Hey look at that, they found you a uniform." He

tugged at my arm where my pilot officer's braids had been sewn.

"Oi! Careful. I've just got this back from the tailor's."

"Well you better send it back." Warwick handed me an envelope. My heart skipped as I rashly jumped to the conclusion that there had been some mistake and my commission was being revoked. With one arm still in a sling I struggled to open the envelope. Aussie tore it from my hands and took the letter out. He held it at arm's length and read out loud.

"Dear Sir, I am directed to inform you that you have been awarded the Distinguished Flying Medal and the following citation will appear in the London Gazette. Pilot Officer James Sommers, D.F.M., Royal Air Force, No. 506 Squadron. Pilot Officer Sommers showed consistent effort and courage. As a fighter pilot his example of courage and resolution has earned great praise." He folded the letter back up. "What a load of bullshit."

I looked at Warwick in utter amazement.

"Better get that back to the tailor and get the ribbon sewn on." He pointed to my top pocket. "But don't get too cocky, old Aussie here got the D.F.C. as well."

Doc shot a glance towards the reception desk.

"Right let's smuggle you out for a drink," he whispered. Via the kitchens we negotiated our way outside to a staff car that Aussie had somehow managed to purloin.

It turned out the squadron had been pulled out of the line for respite a few days after my incident. By pure coincidence they'd been posted to Filton about an hour's drive from the hotel.

We quickly found a decent looking pub and

managed to squeeze in a round of drinks before last orders were called for the afternoon. It was sheer delight to be with those friends again. We laughed and joked, but somehow managed to avoid talking about the war. As I relaxed back in the chair and looked at my three comrades, I felt a familiar tension grow in my stomach. We had been through a lot together.

All too soon our time was up and we were politely asked to leave the saloon bar by a fierce looking landlady. Doc and Warwick headed to the outside toilets while Aussie and I wandered slowly to the car. He offered me a Capstan and lit it for me.

"We lost Freddie I'm afraid." For a moment he disappeared behind the flame from the lighter which flickered in front of my eyes. I breathed in and exhaled.

"When?" I asked.

"A day after you went down." Aussie turned and looked at the low sun which was starting to set. "Doc saw him heading out over the North Sea. The light was fading and a sea mist had sprung up. We don't know if some Jerry had him or he just got lost."

Strangely, I wasn't surprised at the news.

I just hoped it had been quick.

The Article

World in Pictures Magazine, October 1940
Defenders of the skies.
The young men who are turning the tide of this war.

Nestled in a quiet area of the Essex countryside, a grass airfield hums with activity. This is home for the pilots of 506 Squadron Royal Air Force. From here each day they patrol the skies above London looking for Nazi raiders. The well organised air defence system ensures as soon as the enemy is spotted the Hawker Hurricanes of 506 can pounce. The combat is furious, brief and exhausting. But the young men of 506 are always alert.

Picture above: The pilots of 506 Squadron with trophies recovered from enemy aircraft they've destroyed.

Picture right: Pilot Officer Sommers D.F.M. of 506 Squadron. At 21 he has already been declared an Ace, having shot down five enemy aircraft. Two of these were in the same attack.

Postscript

The road in front straightened out. I opened up the throttle and let all four cylinders race. The low autumnal sun strobed across the dashboard as the tall hedgerows flashed by. In the mirror I could see freshly fallen leaves dancing neat circular patterns in the wake of the big Bentley. The year was getting old, the temperature was cold and the days were short.

The tyres bit down hard on the tarmac as the camber of the road twisted into a gentle left hand turn. I crested a hill and the South Downs opened up before me. I eased off the throttle and braked hard into a short gravel layby. The brakes were heavy and I skidded slightly on the loose stone. Mac had always said it was easy to get the car to a hundred miles an hour, but slowing down and stopping was another matter.

After he was killed the Bentley had been laid up at North Weald. His family had no use for it so it was gifted to the pilots of 506. I'd become fond of the old girl and seemed to be the only one of us who could handle the tricky gearbox. I offered to buy the other chaps out of their share. The price was set at twelve pints of beer and I became her owner.

I cut the ignition and the four cylinders rested. I pushed myself out of the driver's seat favouring my right arm as my elbow was still tender. I looked across the magnificent downs and the crimson sun that was setting.

After an extensive examination and a fair bit of poking and prodding I had been declared fit to fly again. I'd spent a week's leave visiting a few old friends and spending time with my family in Oxford.

On the last day I'd dropped by Westminster to see Lucy. Six weeks had passed since Freddie was posted missing.

Lucy had worn a well cut cotton dress with a typically British brave face, but it was easy to see how upset she was. Freddie and her had been very close. In conversation she pondered the idea that he might turn up somewhere, somehow.

On receiving my commission I'd been posted to another squadron. It was disappointing not to be flying with the men I had got to know so well over that intense summer, but a squadron is constantly evolving. 506 and that little wooden crew room in the corner of North Weald no longer belonged to me.

I leant against the Bentley and watched an aircraft in the far distance. I wondered what orders the pilot had been given as its black silhouette crossed the dramatic skyline. I lit a cigarette and spent a few minutes taking in the view. I stretched my legs and flexed my elbow, it felt stiff in the cold air. From the rear of the car I took my Sheepskin flying jacket and pulled it over my uniform. The leather was now soft and supple and fitted well around my shoulders.

I climbed back into the Bentley and lowered myself into the seat. I ran my fingers over the two brass switches and clicked them into position. I pressed the black Bakelite starter button, there was a hiss and then a cough and the 4-cylinder engine came to life. With a flick of another switch the headlights shone forward down the darkening road.

Hand brake off and I eased my foot on the accelerator pedal. A puff of gravel shot up from the rear as the wheels span. A quick turn of the head to check all was clear and I pulled forward onto the road.

Printed in Great Britain
by Amazon